After All...

R.N.F. SKINNER

SilverWood

Published in 2022 by SilverWood Books

SilverWood Books Ltd
14 Small Street, Bristol, BS1 1DE, United Kingdom
www.silverwoodbooks.co.uk

ISBN 978-1-80042-202-5 (paperback)
ISBN 978-1-80042-203-2 (ebook)

British Library Cataloguing in Publication Data
A CIP catalogue record for this book is
available from the British Library

Page design and typesetting by SilverWood Books

R.N.F. (RICHARD) SKINNER has published the novel *Still Crazy…* (SilverWood, 2020) and several poetry collections, as well as composing lyrics for a range of songs including the musical *Bethlehem*! His short stories, well represented in the current collection, have appeared in a range of literary magazines, and have twice gained him a literary award from South West Arts.

While studying for a degree in Natural Sciences from Cambridge University, he was invited to become a member of the famous 'Footlights' club, later co-founding and performing with a cabaret-revue team. He continues to write and perform sketch-based comedy in cabaret, the scripts of some of his sketches are included in the current collection. Following *Still Crazy…* and the current collection *After All…*, he is working on a novella entitled *These Years* and intends to publish in the near future.

He moved from London to Devon in 1975 to focus on his writing whilst working in a variety of jobs, mainly in the mental health sector. In 2012 he was awarded a doctorate from Exeter University for his thesis on religion and evolutionary theory. He lives in Exeter with his wife, three hens, a dog and a cat.

For further information about the books of R.N.F. Skinner, please visit his website at rnfskinner.com

Acknowledgements

'The Mask Factory' was first published in *Pennine Ink*

'Dancing in the Brambles' was first published in *South West Review*

'Shock Treatment' was first published in *Critical Quarterly*

'Deprived Children' was first published in *Odyssey*

'A Change of Mind' received a South-West Arts Literary Award

Many thanks to Gordon Clarke and David Thompson for many helpful comments about several of these items, and especially to Betsy Allen for her unfailing support and encouragement.

My thanks also go to the SilverWood team for their skill, professionalism and friendliness as we have worked on this book together. It's been a great pleasure to have been working with them once again.

Contents

Introduction

The following collection consists of a number of short stories which are (in the main) simply fiction, along with two pieces recounting episodes from my short spell as a psychiatric nursing assistant in the late 1970s, a whimsical observation of patients on the ward of a general hospital in 2021, and a dozen comedy scripts.

One of the stories ('The Lure of the Footlights') features Phil, the male protagonist of my novel *Still Crazy...* (SilverWood 2020). Set in 1969, two years before he first appears in the novel performing cabaret, this story has many autobiographical elements – in particular the episode of his watching the Cambridge Footlights revue at the Edinburgh Festival fringe. It remains in my memory as the most joyously funny evening imaginable, for which I am ever grateful to Clive James (who co-wrote and produced it) and the cast of *An Hour Late*.

The scripts constitute a small selection of comedy sketches written and performed over many years, initially with a cabaret-revue team, Seventh Sense – formerly The Headlights – and in recent years with Gordon Clarke. They have all been performed many times and, mutating as they do from performance to performance, none of them has an entirely fixed script. Each one included, then, is a composite formed from a number of different versions.

Short stories

Wonders to Perform

"It's all pretty straightforward," said the director, a harassed-looking man called Colin in a harassed-looking green jersey. "All you have to do is start shouting *here*." He was pointing at a tatty script, where he'd marked a large, felt-tipped X in the margin. "Ordinary shouting to begin with. There'll be five or six others in different parts of the audience who'll take their cue from you and start shouting as well. Then you have to get louder, more insistent. Remember, you really mean it! You're demanding it."

Arthur nodded. "Yeah, great, I can do that. I'll enjoy doing it! Barabbas!" he shouted suddenly. "Give us Barabbas!"

"Excellent!" said Colin. "And then, here" —he turned over the pages— "this is where you shout—"

"Let 'im 'ave it!" Arthur leapt to his feet. "String 'im up!"

"No! No!" Colin said hastily. "Stick to the script. Don't improvise! They didn't string people up in those days, not the way you mean. Stick to the script."

"Crucify!" Arthur amended loudly. "Crucify 'im! Crucify!"

"That's it!" Colin smiled weakly. "And then, when you've shouted it a few times – six times, say, no more – you stop shouting and sit down again. No more shouting," he emphasised, and with a ballpoint pen scrawled on the script: *shout 'Crucify' 6 times only, then sit down again.* "You keep this script. So you know."

"Crucify," Arthur muttered. Then, louder, "*Crucify* 'im! Crucify *'im*!"

As Colin left him practicing different ways of uttering the words and rejoined the cast, he feared he'd made a mistake in asking Arthur to lead the shouting. "Involve the community," the Rev. Alec Martin, vicar of the church hosting the first of the Holy Week performances, had requested. "Ask some of our lesser-talented brethren to do something. It makes them feel wanted. Arthur, for instance." So Arthur had been asked. But perhaps, Colin now thought, it would have been better if the asking had been more along the lines of "can we use your muscle, Arthur, to shift the piano and those tables?" Or "would you be able to help us get our lighting gear and sound system in place?" But too late now. Arthur was the designated cheerleader of the mob.

Arthur apart, Colin was confident about the casting – Jesus in particular. The role had been given to a member of the troupe who until then had played only minor parts but had expressed himself ready for something meatier. It was his air of quiet authority, cultivated for his day job as Chief Planning Officer at County Hall, that had landed him the leading role.

The casting, however, was not without controversy. "Do you think it wise given what he's just done?" the vicar had asked, referring to a planning application that Jesus, in his Planning Officer incarnation, had recently passed for building an estate of more than 200 houses on the edge of the village. The locals were unamused. "He's a rather controversial figure right now."

"So was Jesus," Colin replied.

"True," the vicar said thoughtfully. "But Jesus was the Messiah, whereas this man seems to think he's actually the Lord God Almighty."

Easter was approaching. Over the years, Colin's amateur but enthusiastic troupe had successfully performed a wide range of plays, from *Blithe Spirit* to *Loot*, from *Arsenic and Old Lace* to *The Crucible*. Last year, such was the regard in which they were held, they had gone on a mini-tour of the surrounding villages with *Murder in the Cathedral*, performing to good audiences and great acclaim in churches, village halls and school halls, but not, regrettably, in the cathedral itself. Colin, keen to rectify this omission, had approached the dean with the suggestion that they repeat their *Murder* triumph in the cathedral, but the dean, newly appointed and keen to flex his decanal muscles after the laxity of the previous administration, had sniffily rejected the idea on the grounds that "We only book professional...er..."

"Murderers?" Colin had boldly interjected.

"Performers," the dean spoke over him.

Not so much deterred by the ecclesiastical rebuff as galvanised, Colin and the troupe had determined to do another tour with performances of the play in Dorothy L. Sayers' drama cycle *The Man Born to be King* which dealt with the trial of Jesus before his crucifixion. Venues were booked, the script adapted, roles cast, and then someone – Jesus? Pilate? Barabbas? – came up with what had seemed at the time to be the bright idea of involving the audience in the scene where Pilate presents Jesus and Barabbas to the crowd and demands to know which one they want to be set free and which to be executed. Though perhaps, Colin thought more than once as rehearsals progressed, the brightness of the idea would have been more honoured in its breach.

Arthur religiously attended rehearsals, which happened to be taking place in the hall of his home village, with the first night due to take place in its mediaeval church. He was present even when the Jesus-with-Pilate-and-the-mob scene was not being rehearsed, sitting at the back and disconcertingly muttering "*Cru*cify 'im! Cruci*fy* 'im! Crucify '*im*!" at random. When that scene *was* on the schedule, he pitched in enthusiastically, sometimes a page too soon, such that Colin had to summon up more and more patience in reminding Arthur when, and when not, to shout. Colin's green jersey grew even more harassed-looking as the days and rehearsals went by. But slowly Arthur started to confine his interjections to the place and wording dictated by the script, and Colin's jersey relaxed.

On the Saturday before Palm Sunday, with the first performance to take place on Monday, Arthur did lend his muscles to piano-shifting in the church, then practically single-handedly brought in the lighting gear and helped set it up, proving tireless in that capacity. The dress rehearsal then proceeded well enough without being perfect – which in theatrical circles, Colin reminded them, is considered ideal, with any hiccups regarded as being a safeguard against the dangers of over-confidence. It was not, however, Arthur who contributed the hiccups providing the necessary antidote to perfection, but Caiaphas the high priest forgetting his lines twice and a Roman soldier exiting stage left instead of stage right, marching smartly into the scenery and swearing in fluent Anglo-Saxon.

The publicity was efficient, and tickets had sold well for the entire run. First night, and the church was packed. The whole village and more seemed to be present. Arthur was in his designated seat, and Colin saw with relief that the half-dozen other planted members of the mob were also in place, scattered throughout the audience. One of them, a churchwarden, was sitting next to Arthur with instructions to restrain him if he displayed any tendency to leap up and start shouting prematurely. An outburst during the Sanhedrin's interview with Jesus, for example, would not only contradict the biblical account but also be, in Colin's view, a theatrical mortal sin.

The play began. The performers were all hardened amateur actors, good at projecting – even overprojecting – their voices, almost word-perfect, reasonably adept at knowing what to do with their hands when making a speech, and well schooled in not absent-mindedly picking noses or scratching backsides when the spotlight, real or virtual, was not trained on them.

Colin, from his vantage point deep in the wings from where he could survey the house, perceived with considerable satisfaction the mesmeric effect the drama was clearly having on the audience. He could tell by their unwavering collective gaze and intent facial expressions that they were hooked, rapt, emotionally stirred by being transported to first-century Jerusalem. Even though everyone present knew perfectly well the outcome of the Easter story, such knowledge, like disbelief, had been willingly suspended; they were actually living through those events, experiencing them emotionally for the very first time. They, the audience, had become the inhabitants of and visitors to Jerusalem at the time of the Roman occupation when the controversial man from Nazareth was causing a considerable stir. That was the power of theatre – and it never ceased to amaze and delight Colin how a good play well performed could insinuate itself into the psyches of audience after audience…

As the scene approached of Pilate offering the mob the choice between Jesus and Barabbas, Colin's anxiety suddenly resurfaced. He could see Arthur in his seat, script in hand, mouth working; but would he start the shouting for Barabbas as instructed and as he had been endlessly rehearsed? Or in the heat of the moment would he leap straight to the much more exciting cry of 'Crucify!'? Would Arthur unwittingly break the spell? Snatch the audience back to the twenty-first century?

The critical scene arrived. Pilate, a painter and decorator when he wasn't governing Judea and executing rebels, was centre stage, with two or three minions around, including the Roman guard. Jesus stood imperturbably stage left, Barabbas scowlingly stage right. Pilate stepped forward and addressed the audience directly.

"Which of the two do you want released?" he demanded, gesturing. "Barabbas the robber? Or Jesus, whom you call Christ?"

There was a microsecond's pause. Colin sweated.

Then, abruptly, "Barabbas!" Arthur howled. "Give us Barabbas!" Perhaps a mite louder than he had been rehearsed to howl, but *they were the right words in the right order* delivered *at the right time* – that was all that mattered. Colin closed his eyes, leaned back and exhaled in relief.

The churchwarden next to Arthur had joined in, as had the others planted in the audience. "Barabbas!" the cry resounded. "Barabbas!" And Barabbas, a black-bearded, beetle-browed teacher of tai chi who revelled in always playing the villain in the troupe's various productions, smirked his best villainous smirk before being escorted off the stage.

Jesus, at Pilate's gesture, was now brought centre stage by the Roman guard as the cries for Barabbas died away. Tall, weary-looking but standing erect, he barely blinked once, a trick he claimed to have learned by studying Robert Powell in Zeffirelli's *Jesus of Nazareth*.

"And what," Pilate, all menacing tones and oily smiles, now demanded of the audience, "shall I do with Jesus called Christ?"

There was a pause. Colin's eyes widened – surely Arthur hadn't missed his second cue? Surely he hadn't frozen? Surely he—

"Crucify!" Arthur bellowed, leaping to his feet and pointing a furious finger at Jesus. "Crucify 'im!"

Immediately "Crucify!" was echoed elsewhere in the church as another figure jumped up, another finger pointed.

"Crucify!" called out the churchwarden next to Arthur in an emollient tone of voice, which implied an additional 'if that's all right with the rest of you'.

"*Cru*cify 'im!" Arthur bellowed again. "Crucify *'im*!"

"Crucify! Crucify him! Crucify! Crucify!" The call now came from all parts of the building, bounced off the walls, a roar of overlapping voices as more and more people sprang to their feet. "Crucify! Crucify!"

A regular chant set up. On stage, Jesus remained impassive but Pilate began to look nervous. His eyes shifted to the wings, where Colin was frowning. There were only seven nominated members of the mob to do the shouting, but now more than a dozen members of the audience were joining in. Now a score, and now even more. Real audience participation. Too much participation. Far too much; and the play needed to move on. The mob had to settle back down. The chanting had to stop.

But the chanting continued. More voices joined in. Soon half the audience were on their feet, more than half, three-quarters…some chanting in unison, others interjecting variants of the cry in a kind of crucifixion counterpoint.

"Crucify! Cruuuuuuuucify! Crucify!"

Jesus started to lose his impassive look. He was seen to lick his lips nervously.

"Cruuuuuuuucify! Crucify! Cruuuuuuuucify!"

The entire audience had risen. The entire audience chanted. The entire audience demanded the crucifixion of Jesus called Christ. All of them. All, that is, except for Arthur. Arthur had been well rehearsed. Having shouted the requisite six times, he had sat down again, and had already taken out his mobile phone to record the unfolding events.

"Crucify! Crucify! Crucify!" the entire audience (less the seated one) was chanting. "Cruuuuuuuucify!"

Like something out of *Invasion of the Body Snatchers*, the audience now started moving out of their seats, chanting, each chant emphasised by the drawing back of their arms then the flinging of them forward again with extended, accusatory index fingers.

"Crucify! Crucify! Crucify!"

"Christ Almighty!" Pilate the painter and decorator was heard to mutter, overturning two thousand years of Christian teaching concerning the beliefs of the governor of Judea. "What the hell are they doing?"

"Cruuuuuuuucify!"

"Bloody hell!" said Jesus in turn, his air of divine authority plummeting to zero. "Let's get out of here!"

The Roman guard, deploying his considerable stock of Anglo-Saxon swear words in one almighty ungrammatical and anachronistic outburst, and already disappearing in the direction of the emergency exit, was now rapidly followed by Pilate, Jesus and the rest of the onstage cast.

It was unfortunate that during the shifting of the piano the parochial Health and Safety Officer had not been in attendance, for the emergency exit had been and remained partly blocked by the instrument, despite the warning notice *Keep Clear At All Times* – which, admittedly, was now difficult to read with a piano parked in front of it. Colin and the Roman guard sweated to shift the piano out of the way, but one of the castors proved recalcitrant and jammed, causing the instrument suddenly to swivel awkwardly and knock over Barabbas the tai chi teacher, whose response was more in keeping with the former role than the latter. Pilate continued to deviate sharply from the gospel accounts with his plaintive calling upon Jesus to save him.

"Unbar the door!" someone yelled, reverting as though by instinct to the troupe's production of *Murder in the Cathedral*.

"Crucify! Crucify! Crucify!" the still advancing mob yelled.

The Roman guard responded with yet more unbiblical Anglo-Saxon invective.

"Cruuuuuuuucify!" howled the crowd.

Jesus yanked down on the emergency exit's release bar which had been revealed by the swivelling of the piano. The door swung open...

The rest of the tour was cancelled. Colin's green jersey never recovered. Arthur uploaded the video from his phone onto the internet, where it went viral. Jesus took long-term sick leave from County Hall and entered intensive therapy. His replacement as Planning Officer, undertaking a review of several of his recent controversial decisions, quickly discovered evidence that questionable procedures had been followed with regard to the housing scheme near the village, along with insufficient public consultation and a suspicious family connection between Jesus and the CEO of the firm of would-be developers. He lost no time in rescinding the planning permission.

When this decision became known, the Rev. Alec Martin exchanged high fives with the churchwarden, and together they planned a special thanksgiving service in the church. The entire village attended, including atheists, agnostics and New Agers, and all were treated to a stirring sermon based on the quotation 'God moves in a mysterious way His wonders to perform'.

"Though sometimes, as we all know," the vicar concluded in a hushed, conspiratorial tone of voice, "He needs a little help."

The Mask Factory

"My car's broken down," the man called Travers said, "and I can't get a signal." He waved his mobile phone at her.

The young woman behind the desk held up her right hand while muttering into the little ball microphone attached to her headset. All Travers could hear her say was a series of letters and numbers. She then nodded, evidently listening to a reply through her headphones. "The Controller will be down presently," she informed Travers, smiling sweetly.

"There's no need for all that," Travers said quickly. "All I want is to use a phone so I can call the breakdown people."

"Please, do take a seat," she said.

"Just a phone," Travers reiterated.

The young woman's smile had become forced. "Take a seat," she insisted.

Travers hesitated, then turned away in annoyance. She was obviously a jobsworth, incapable of making the smallest decision by herself but had to refer to a higher authority.

Too agitated to sit on one of the plush armchairs in the vast atrium, he wandered about looking for some indication of what sort of place he was in. Hell of a morning. Early start, distant destination, wilds of Dartmoor, then the damned satnav had packed up, followed by the descent – or possibly ascent – of a swirling mist blotting out the old moorland signposts at a series of road junctions, and shortly after that the car grinding to a halt. No phone signal. This large complex of buildings, surrounded by high wire fencing topped by what looked like barbed wire, presumably some high-security government outpost along the lines of GCHQ, had loomed out of the mist a few minutes earlier, and he had risked walking back to it clutching his old-fashioned road atlas in the hopes of finding someone like a security guard who could let him use a phone, or at least point him in the right direction for getting help. Surprisingly, though, the security of the place appeared to be negligible, and he had walked unchallenged through wide open gates into the compound and then into the building itself.

But he realised as he wandered around the atrium that he hadn't seen any boards or nameplates indicating the function of the building, and now, on the various glass-topped metal-framed tables dotted around, there were none of the company brochures and reports and magazines and the like one would normally expect to find. Odd.

"Mr Travers?" a soft voice said behind him.

He turned round. An elderly man with thin grey hair and a face like that of a melting snowman was holding out his hand to him.

"Er, yes," said Travers as his hand was shaken.

"Welcome to the Mask Factory, Mr Travers," the man said. "I have the privilege of being the Controller here."

"Do you?" said Travers, puzzled by the use of his name. "Are you?"

"Indeed. Now, do come this way. I'm sure you will be very interested to see the running of our establishment. It's not often we have the opportunity to explain ourselves."

As the Controller hustled him out of the atrium and along the corridor, Travers again tried explaining that all he wanted was the use of a phone to call the breakdown services, and to be shown on the map where exactly he was. What this establishment was that he had stumbled across in the middle of the moor no longer interested him.

The Controller, however, was still speaking. "The nerve centre of our entire enterprise," he said, "is, naturally, the Repository."

"Oh. Is it?"

"Indeed it is. Now, as you would expect, in the Repository we have stored every possible human response there can ever be."

"Oh, ah?" Travers panted. The Controller was setting a challenging pace.

"You are no doubt wondering exactly *which* responses?"

Not really, Travers was thinking.

"And the answer is: *every* response! However subtle or gross, whatever has been or could be felt, experienced, conceived or manifested by a human being throughout the existence of humanity is contained in our Repository. Conceal and reveal: the purpose of the masks is to permit the balance between concealing and revealing those responses. Our masks, you understand, are the masks without which human beings could not exist. Remember that."

As they went along many corridors and passages, the Controller continuing at a brisk pace, Travers realised that the style of architecture and decoration were familiar. The archways, the large spaces, the abstract designs on the walls, the very proportions all reminded him of buildings he had seen, and been into, on a trip along the Silk Road. So graceful. There'd been no getting lost *there*; the planning by the tour company had been meticulous. But back *here*, and he gets lost on bloody Dartmoor.

They passed numerous archways which, Travers could see, led through to vast areas beyond, but they went in none until they arrived at and entered a huge hall. The walls curved smoothly away with eye-baffling contours: the far end virtually out of sight; the ceiling immeasurably high; and in the hall countless little bays, in each of which sat a figure on a chair, a large cushion or a thick rug. The gentle susurration of the rhythmical breathing of the hall's innumerable inhabitants pervaded the space.

"What's all this about?" said Travers, intrigued despite himself.

"This is the Hall of the Shapers," said the Controller. "The process of creating and sustaining a mask has several stages. First, the mask is to be designed. This is a task of great skill, carried out by the Shapers. It is the Shaper who first conceives the subtle balance of elements from which emerges a unique mask. It depends on the blend and balance of elements: gesture and word, tone and timbre, poise and position; the fleeting glance, the curl of a finger, the inflexion of voice, the avoided thought; the ache in the tooth and the flicker of the eye; the twitch of muscle and the rising blush; the vein throbbing on the back of the hand, the flare of the nostril...all are contained, of course, in our Repository. I could enumerate countless upon countless elements and still not exhaust the physical responses alone. Yet each mask is a blend of the physical and emotional, the spiritual and mental – I use these categories for convenience, you understand? The physical and emotional, spiritual and mental are ultimately one and the same. We recognise no true distinction.

"The Shapers draw upon all these elements to ensure that the dual functions of concealing and revealing are fulfilled. Any mask design which conceals but does not sufficiently reveal will destroy the person within. Any mask which reveals but does not conceal will destroy others. We are the mediators and the filters of reality – each mask must maintain a subtle balance. Come."

They pass through a doorway back into the corridor. The Controller indicates another opening and they enter a second hall, seemingly identical to the first.

"The Fashioners," the Controller says. "In here the fashioning of the masks is undertaken."

Travers looks at the postures, the faces, the expressions of the Fashioners. Silent, still and focused. The same susurration as in the first hall.

"Working with the designs developed by the Shapers, the Fashioners bring the masks into reality, employing the most subtle of essences. Theirs is the most delicate of tasks, for each mask has to be a unity – it must fully express the meaning for which it has been designed and created. It possesses – no, it *is* – an intrinsic internal harmony which the Fashioner has to realise. Only the Fashioners themselves have full cognizance of their procedures, and that is purely through experience. But without their constant fashioning, the masks would remain speculative, insubstantial."

Travers is taken to more halls, all apparently identical to the first two, where the work of the Scrutinisers, the Deliverers and the Reclaimers is explained. Then, although expecting yet another hall, he finds himself conducted into a small, circular room. The Controller's office.

"Be seated," says the Controller. "Now, Mr Travers, do you have any questions?"

Travers leans forward. "What's it all for?" he demands.

"Conceal and reveal – remember? We in the Mask Factory are the mediators of reality. Masks are the stuff of existence. Indeed, one might say that they *are* existence."

Travers is silent for several seconds. He is not thinking. He is not able to think. He has even forgotten the reason for his entering the building in the first place.

"Would I be right," the Controller asks, "in assuming that you still have a measure of doubt?"

The power of thought returns. "You could say that," Travers nods.

"And what would remove that doubt?"

Travers stares at the Controller. "The Repository. You claimed that something called the Repository is the nerve centre of your entire enterprise. But all you've shown me has been halls full of people doing nothing. What about this Repository of yours?"

"Indeed. I have not shown you the Repository. Were I to show it to you, you would be convinced?"

"Try me."

The Controller sighs. "I can certainly show you the Repository. But I caution you that it might not be all that wise. Think of what it means if my claim is true – and I assure you it is. The Repository contains every human feeling, emotion, affect and response – past, present and future. Are you able to grasp the significance of that? Will you be able to bear entering the Repository? Are you prepared for such an experience?"

"Try me," Travers repeats.

"Very well. I congratulate you." The Controller stands up and motions with his hand towards an area of the wall. The image of a door appears. It wavers, as though being projected onto a slowly undulating screen; then it becomes fully door.

"The entrance to the Repository. You have one final chance to withdraw. There will be no disgrace in doing so."

"I wish to see."

"The door is not locked. You may enter."

Travers takes hold of the handle of the door and turns it. The door swings silently open. He is briefly aware of a swirling fog as he steps forward into the Repository.

He looks around. This, then, is the Repository, in which is to be found the entire range of human responses. But he is no longer indoors, but back on the moor itself. He turns. No sign of any door, nor indeed any building. Just moorland, with a few sparse trees and granite outcrops. The mist has dispersed, and he can see the road two or three hundred yards away. As he starts to walk towards his car, he takes out and checks his mobile phone. A signal. When he gets into his car and turns the key, it starts immediately.

And the satnav is once again working. It tells him to do a U-turn when possible.

What's in a Name?

"Do you really want a coffee," she said, opening the front door, "or shall we go straight to bed?"

Although startled by the directness of the question, he managed not to show it. He had indeed supposed that the offer of coffee on reaching her flat was simply the traditional preliminary manoeuvre to enable each of them to check out indirectly the level of keenness or indifference of the other about the possibility of sex, rather than it being a serious attempt to elicit attitudes towards caffeine usage, but he hadn't previously encountered such a complete refusal to play the coy game of preludial coffee-drinking and small talk.

One problem he immediately faced before answering was that although he did want to go to bed with her, he was also actually desperate for something non-alcoholic to drink. Tea, though, for preference, not coffee. Not that saying he would like such a drink would necessarily preclude subsequent sex, unless she took offence at what she might interpret as an intention on his part to avoid bedding her – but the two activities of tea-drinking and love-making were not in themselves logically mutually exclusive...well, no: strictly speaking, he supposed, they *were* mutually exclusive in that you couldn't carry them out *literally* simultaneously, otherwise at the critical moment the tea would go all over the place, not only scalding what shouldn't be scalded but also necessitating a change of bedclothes and a sponging down of the mattress, though admittedly that could be true of sex on its own; but tea as a preliminary to sex, as an interval drink during sex, and as a post-coital refreshment to signify that sex was, for the time being at least, over – all these scenarios were perfectly possible, desirable even. Which meant that within the same time span both activities could perfectly well be carried out, hence demolishing any presupposition that tea and sex constituted a fundamental either/or. But still, he would like a cup of tea.

A second problem to face was his current status. Only three months had passed since he and Zoe had parted company. Amicably enough, but it had resulted in his being celibate since then – five months of celibacy in total, given the lead-in period to the separation. He missed Zoe, and since then had held out hopes for a reconciliation, though there had been no positive responses from her when he had tentatively tried to explore the possibility. Too tentatively, perhaps? For him now to get sexually involved with another woman would mark a turning point, even if it proved to be just a one-night stand; it would, to his mind, signify his abandoning such hopes of getting back with Zoe. It didn't *have* to have that significance, but he knew that to him it would.

But the third, and by far the most urgent, problem facing him was that he still couldn't remember her name.

He could remember being *told* her name when they were introduced to each other at the party, but to be told a name is a long way from knowing what that name is three hours later – even though, or more likely *because*, for quite a large proportion of the time they had been engaged in kissing, cuddling and, to use the old-fashioned term he rather liked, canoodling. Naturally he hadn't needed her name while they were doing all that, and by the time they'd decided to leave the party together, just as it was winding down in any case, her name had been erased from his memory. Not outright, though. It left behind a trace: he was pretty sure her name began with an A. But it was not Anne; not Antonia; not Andrea; not Alice nor Alison; not Abigail… Or did it begin with a K? He had been silently going through the alphabet ever since they had stopped kissing, cuddling and canoodling and decided to leave, and both A and K had given him a little flick of significance… Karen? Katherine? Katie? He had hoped that, as they left, someone would have called out to her in valediction: "Cheerio, A—!" or "See you, K—!" as the case may be. But no one did call out to her. He had resumed going through the alphabet repeatedly as they drove back here to her place, at the same time trying to maintain a casual conversation with her about his and her tastes in music, but with no greater enlightenment. Anastasia? Adele? Anita? Kathleen? Katrina?

He couldn't now, of course, just ask her outright. Had he asked to be reminded five minutes, say, after first being told, that would have been acceptable. Do it with a self-deprecating laugh and say, "Sorry, memory like a sieve, what did you say your name is?" during the time when they had still been exchanging opening pleasantries. Or, bolder, "Sorry, what did you say your name is? I got distracted by your gorgeousness and didn't take it in!" But by the time she was sitting – or rather, wriggling – on his lap, too late.

The sitting and wriggling had come about because, having danced for some time both energetically and smoochily, they had quit the dance floor to discover that only one empty chair was available – one on which she had presciently left a shawl. "That's all right," she'd said gaily. "You sit down – go on, and I'll sit on your lap!" And, sitting (wriggling) on his lap, an arm round his neck, she had kissed him on the mouth, a long, slow, sexy kiss. He'd soon started to wonder if she'd do a Mae West and ask if it were a gun – or was it handkerchief? – in his pocket, or was he just...? But she hadn't asked. She'd been too busy kissing and being kissed. When, occasionally, by unspoken mutual agreement, they had come up for air, it hadn't seemed appropriate to ask the name of the woman he was kissing, cuddling and canoodling with. And he certainly couldn't ask now, half an hour or more after the end of his extended k, c and c with...Audrey? Agatha? Angela? Keeley? Kirsty?

All these considerations did not present themselves to him in a sequence of thoughts, each to be pondered on and resolved before he could reply to her 'coffee or bed?' question, but they came rather in a complete block of realisation, like a landscape at night being suddenly lit up *in toto* by a brilliant flash of lightning. Neither did he deliberately and consciously verbalise the dilemma to himself and try to analyse it, for it lay beyond words – except for the persistently erroneous substitutes for her elusive name. So it was that only a fraction of a second passed before he answered her by saying, "I wouldn't mind a *tea* if that's okay, and then, er—"

He was uncertain how to finish the sentence, but she saved him the trouble by interrupting with a breezy: "Tea in bed, then you in me! That's cool!"

He followed her through to the kitchen, where she busied herself with kettle and mugs and teabags and milk. Then she turned and caught him ogling her. "Bedroom's first on the right," she said, smiling and pointing at the kitchen door. "Bathroom's next to it." She turned back to the tea-making, and wiggled her bottom.

He entered the bedroom. Pastel colours, a large bed – larger than an ordinary double – and tidy enough, with a few items of clothing draped over the back of a chair. A fluffy white bathrobe on the back of the door. He switched on the bedside light, then at the window he pulled on the cord to close the blinds before turning back to inspect the room some more. Surely he could find something in here to resolve the problem of her name. But nothing on the walls helped – no certificates, awards, group photos with names attached. No greeting or birthday cards or the like from friends or family on the dressing table or on the shelf cluttered with ornaments and other knick-knacks. No letters lying about with giveaway salutations or envelopes addressed to her. Promisingly, though, there were a couple of rows of books, but a quick inspection of several paperbacks picked out at random showed that she was apparently not someone who scribbled her name in books.

While he was checking another book – a raunchy-looking novel by someone he'd not heard of – she came into the bedroom carrying two mugs. More significantly, she was considerably less dressed than she had been earlier, stripped down as she now was to red bra and knickers. She put down the two mugs on a side table and came across to him.

"Why are you," she said, putting an arm round his neck, "still dressed?" And, putting her mouth on his, she kissed him even more sexily than she had at the party, while her free hand went to the front of his trousers and started massaging him. He was only semi-aroused. Kelly? Kylie? Kitty? Agnes? Albertine? Amanda?

She stopped kissing him, removed her hand and stepped back. "I need to go next door. Won't be a minute! See you in bed!" And as she left the bedroom, she reached behind her back, undid the bra strap and allowed the bra to fall to the floor. Again she wiggled her bottom. She had a bottom worth wiggling, but no amount of wiggling would reveal her name, and the nagging embarrassment of his forgetfulness was proving fatal to having fun with her in bed. Alexandria? Anthea? Agnetha? Kay? Kerry? Kimberley? Krystal?

As soon as he heard the bathroom door click shut, he acted. Moving as quickly and quietly as possible he returned to the kitchen, collected his jacket, then headed for the front door. Thank God it opened easily and with little noise. Out. Shut the door. Through the lobby to the main entrance. Outside. Run to car, pressing car remote. Side lights flashing. Into car and, moments later, away down the road.

She thought she'd heard something. Coming out of the bathroom, where her red knickers were now lying on the floor, and finding the bedroom empty, she darted into the front room just in time to see the car pulling away. Sorrowfully she returned to the bedroom, pulled on her fluffy white bathrobe and sat on the bed, wondering what she had done wrong.

He'd been really lovely and fun and sensitive and sexy, and would surely have been great in bed. The last few months had been so full on, dealing with her father's complicated estate while simultaneously studying for her Master's, that she desperately needed a break, with some fun thrown in. It would have been wonderful if she could have had an uninhibited romp with…

She shook her head slowly. An uninhibited romp with…with…an uninhibited romp with… No, no good, she still couldn't remember it… An uninhibited romp with whatever-his-name-was…

Dancing in the Brambles

We never discovered precisely how Alan Hay escaped from the ward, but the likelihood is that one of us on the nursing staff, having let some visitors in or out, failed to check that the door had shut properly. A not uncommon oversight, for the door was supposedly self-locking but on occasions it failed to latch. Alan, lurking in the vicinity and noticing the mistake, was not one to pass by such an opportunity. He bided his time, then when the coast was clear he slipped out and away.

That is conjecture, but what is certain is that at half past two in the afternoon, when someone asked if Alan had been seen recently, we all answered "No". A search of the ward failed to reveal him, and on talking the matter over we came to the conclusion that he had last been around just after lunch. Over an hour ago. He could be, and quite probably was, literally miles away by now.

Into motion went the standard search procedure. All other wards were informed, the hospital grounds were checked, and when the results proved negative higher authorities were notified. This ultimately meant the police. They were told that a patient had escaped from the locked ward of the psychiatric hospital. He was tall and skinny, with long legs and brown curly hair. He had on a pair of blue jeans held up by red braces, a brown sports jacket, a pale blue shirt with no tie, and a straw hat with a large hole in the crown. He would almost certainly be carrying a large tatty copy of the *Guinness Book of Records*.

Our fears were not for the safety of the general public – for Alan was no mad axeman or multiple rapist or pyromaniac – but for Alan himself. In common with most of the patients in the hospital he could not cope with the outside world; he had to be protected from it as much as it from him. He might easily be frightened, and then be a danger to himself. That, at least, was the generally received wisdom.

Medically he was diagnosed as schizophrenic. In reality this meant he suffered from delusions and hallucinations; he went round talking out loud and arguing – sometimes with himself, sometimes with inanimate objects. Walls spoke to him, and presumably made statements he could not agree with, for on occasions he would prance in front of a wall like a shying horse, then strike it repeatedly with his forehead. Not gentle taps but hard blows, time and time again, until one expected the wall to cave in or his head to crack open. Once, having thus chastised a wall, he attacked a perfectly innocent chair, explaining afterwards that he had heard two separate voices. His head-hitting episodes never resulted in any bruising.

Notions of height and age obsessed him. "I'm seven feet nine inches tall!" he would suddenly proclaim, adding somewhat wistfully, "I used to be ten feet tall. Ten feet tall!" His eyes, large and bright, would swivel in their sockets; he would grin broadly, revealing his carious teeth, and then chuckle. Or he would thrust a newspaper cutting under the nose of one of the nurses, point a bony, nicotined finger at a photograph of some personage and solemnly intone, "Eighty-six years old!" or "He's ninety-three next birthday!" His ambition was to live to be a hundred, thus beating his grandfather who, he told us, "was ninety-nine years old when he died!" It was this fascination with such matters that had led to his being bought the *Guinness Book of Records*, and often he could be seen poring over its pages, muttering in admiration at the marvels of stature and longevity recorded therein.

He had a girlfriend, Hilda, on Ward 8, whom he visited from time to time, though it had to be under escort. Hilda suffered from advanced dementia. Once when he was taken to see her, she played hard to get. Undeterred, Alan sat with his arm round her shoulders, talking to her in his peculiarly intent but random fashion. He elicited no response, but when it was time to go he stood up and assured her with earnest dignity, "Alan still loves you, Hilda, Alan still loves you."

This, then, was the man who had absconded. His reality and our reality did not coincide, but he was no fearsome creature, no subhuman beast. Perhaps had he been able to live in a world where his form of reality was the norm he would have been in no danger; but he didn't, and he was.

As it happened, he did not remain at large for long. When we arrived for duty the next morning he was, indeed, still missing, but an hour or so later the internal telephone rang and the message came through that Mr Hay had been returned to the hospital and was at that very moment on course for the ward. The police had found him on the outskirts of a village some ten miles away.

A few minutes later the door opened and in walked Alan, accompanied by the nursing officer. He wandered into the day room as if nothing had happened, grinned, asked for a cigarette, and looked none the worse for his night out. He hadn't eaten, so a breakfast was rescued for him.

Later that morning he had to have a bath, partly because he had missed out the previous evening – his regular bath night – and partly because a doctor wanted to give him a once-over. Though he was perfectly capable of washing himself, I, in accordance with normal practice, was detailed to keep an eye on him.

"So where did you get to, Alan?" I asked, lounging on a chair in the bathroom.

He momentarily paused in his ablutions and frowned intensely.

"A field," he said suddenly, as though the answer to a previously insoluble problem had just flashed through his mind. "There was a field. I had to get through the brambles."

"What – to get out of the field?"

"No!" He shook his head impatiently. "To get in. I had to get into the field. And these brambles, they were…" He broke off and looked up at the ceiling, frowning and muttering, "They were eight feet tall! No! They were…" He raised his right arm in a parody of a Nazi salute. "They were twice as tall as me!"

"That's pretty tall, Alan."

"Yes," he nodded vigorously. "*Twice* as *tall* as *me*! And I fell over two times getting through them, then almost three – I fell over two times, then another three, another four. I fell over," he tried again, "two times, then another four times. That's right. They were *twice* as *tall* as *me*!"

He looked at me and grinned. Not a grin of malice, but one that spoke of a secret joke, a huge, secret delight. Then the frown returned. "I told them, 'Leave me alone!' I said. 'Leave me alone!' Then there was the bull."

"What bull?"

"There was a bull in the field. It nearly got me when I was dancing in the brambles. Dancing in the brambles." The phrase took his fancy and he repeated it several times, his eyes flicking from side to side. It seemed so important to him that he had been dancing in the brambles.

"It was a schizophrenic bull," he continued. "It heard voices. In its head. Did *I* make it schizophrenic? 'Mooo!' it went. 'Mooo!' And I had this feeling of intense..." (I expected him to say 'fear') "...misery! It could have *mashed* me when I was dancing in the brambles."

"But you managed to get away?"

"I got to the other side. There was another field. I think there was another field. There were some geese – eight geese. They came for me." He paused and then added, "I found this hay barn and had a piss in it."

"Did you sleep in there?"

Alan looked doubtful and resumed his washing. "I suppose so," he muttered. "Yes – no – I don't know. But that bull!"

He volunteered no more information, but asked me if he had any scratches on his face. I could see one or two, and several on his shoulders; all of them looked superficial. He dried himself and dressed, then went off to be properly examined by the doctor, who pronounced him physically fit and healthy.

He had, in recounting his experiences, talked like a man who has awoken from a very confusing dream, the elements of which presented themselves to his waking consciousness in distorted, wayward fashion, eluding description. As if a picture had been cut up, and the resulting jigsaw puzzle reassembled haphazardly, with no regard for the original picture. Pieces missing, transposed, inverted, overlapping. Perhaps all reality is like that for Alan. Perhaps when he bangs his head against a wall he is not only trying to still the voices but also to jerk the jigsaw pieces back to their true positions.

Maybe one day he'll succeed. But until then he will continue to consult the *Guinness Book of Records*, converse with unseen colloquists, attack walls and – who knows? – remember the time when he went dancing in the brambles.

Shock Treatment

At ten o'clock Geoff and I left the ward and walked along the corridors. Geoff, who was twenty-eight, had been a patient on the ward for several years. He regularly smashed windows. A few weeks previously he had thrust his head through one of the dormitory windows, and when the night staff had pulled him free he had been jabbing his neck down repeatedly onto the jagged edge and shouting, "I must! I must!" Yet again he had been prescribed a course of electroconvulsive therapy.

I'd read that ECT had come into use decades ago, following on from an alleged observation that people suffering from epilepsy did not suffer from depression. So, the argument had run, if someone could be induced to have epileptic-type fits by pumping a brief burst of electricity through their brain, then depression would be banished. "Of course, it's not true," one of the senior nurses had told me when I'd asked about it. "People with epilepsy do get depressed." But ECT was still part of the psychiatric armoury.

Geoff was smartly dressed, as though attending a job interview. He marched along the corridors with a determined look on his face. One sidepiece of his spectacles was broken, and the piece of sticking plaster holding it on had darkened to a shade approximating to the rest of the black frame.

"D'you think ECT does you any good?" I asked him.

"Suppose it must do," he said in his gormless voice, "otherwise the doc wouldn't have said I had to have it, would he?"

"You've had a lot in your time."

"Yeah, suppose I have."

"You don't mind it?"

"Nah. It's summat to do, ain't it? I'm on a course of ten this time. This one's me seventh."

"Has it helped?"

"I ain't broken any windows recently, have I?"

It struck me that shoving electricity through someone's brain was a strange way to go about safeguarding windows. But at least it gave him something to do – or rather, it gave him something to have done to him.

"But does it stop you feeling depressed?" I asked.

"The best part of it is afterwards," he said, "when, you know, you can't remember anything. It makes everything go cloudy for a bit and stops you thinking. Gives you a break. I suppose if I have enough of it I'll get better, won't I?"

"If you hit a window hard enough it'll turn into strawberry jam," I said.

We reached the ECT ward and I handed Geoff's medical notes to the sister in charge. Several patients from other wards had already arrived, accompanied by nurses. One frail old lady was clutching the arm of a student nurse and repeatedly asking her to look after her teeth.

"But you haven't got any false teeth," the nurse repeated patiently. "You've done very well. You've really looked after your teeth well. They're all your own, aren't they?"

"But they're always telling me to take them out," the old lady said querulously.

"That's only for people who've got false teeth. You haven't, have you?"

The nurse caught my eye and gave a conspiratorial wink. I responded with a quick grin.

Leaving Geoff sitting with the other patients in the little waiting room outside the main part of the ward, I went into where the beds were. A long, rectangular room, it was clean and unfussy, lit by several large windows with yellow curtains, and contained eight beds, four jutting out into the centre of the ward from each of the two long side walls. The nursing sister, a diminutive Chinese woman, was bustling about, preparing the trolley and equipment in time for the arrival of the doctor, who would administer the shocks. On the trolley was a black metallic box with several switches and dials. It was plugged into a wall socket, and from it emerged two coils of flex, each terminating in a short black rod with a disc an inch or so in diameter attached to the end. These were the electrodes through which the electric current would be transmitted to the temples of the patients.

Along with two or three other nurses, I was told to prepare the beds. An incontinence sheet was laid on each bed, a blanket put on top of the sheet, and another blanket placed in readiness at the head of the bed. A pillow was placed on each bed at its foot. The patients would be lying on the beds the wrong way round, with their heads towards the gangway down the centre of the room, so that the trolley could easily be trundled along and the shocks administered efficiently. There was something about it that strongly resembled a production line.

"Get them in, please," the sister said when seven of the beds were prepared. The eighth was not needed. "Make sure they remove spectacles, false teeth, jewellery, watches and so on. Make sure they haven't got anything in their pockets like a comb or keys which could injure them when they fit."

The patients trooped in. Geoff, an old hand, sat on the bed assigned to him and made himself ready without any prompting from me. He was far more familiar with the routine than I was. He removed his shoes, took off his jacket and tie, loosened the belt on his trousers, then swung himself up onto the bed and lay down. I partly covered him with the second blanket.

"I'll keep me specs on a bit longer," he said, "until the doc gets here. And all me teeth are me own!"

"Nothing in your pockets?"

"Nope. I need a thing for me wrist, though. You know, with me name on it."

"Oh, right. Thanks for reminding me."

I wrote his name on a small slip of paper and inserted it into a plastic bracelet, which he then fastened round his wrist.

"In case you forget who I am," he joked.

The patients were all on their beds, blankets covering them, awaiting the arrival of the doctor. The sister fiddled with the machine, then flicked through the patients' notes. She looked at her watch, walked smartly from the room, and returned almost immediately with the doctor. He was a very tall man in his mid-fifties, with old-fashioned Teddy boy sideburns. He strode in.

The doctor spent several minutes looking at the notes. A nurse checked the hypodermic needles and the drugs.

Geoff wiggled his toes and said he wished the doc would get a move on. The frail old lady was still moaning about her teeth.

"All right," said the doctor at last, coming up to Geoff's bed. "Let's get the show on the road. You're the first now – Geoff Stove, isn't it?"

"It's Stone," said Geoff. "Geoff Stone."

"So it is," said the doctor, consulting the notes again, adding with a laugh, "Dreadful writing some doctors have, eh? Part of our training, you know, how to write illegibly. Now then, this is your seventh, isn't it?"

"Yeah," said Geoff. "Three more after this."

"Okay then. Glasses off. That's it. Feel all right?"

"Yeah, thank you," Geoff said politely, handing me his glasses.

"Good! All right, could someone find a vein, please?"

The nurse responded. The injection Geoff received consisted of a short-term general anaesthetic and a muscle relaxant. The latter was to diminish, and preferably eradicate, the violent muscular spasms which would occur in its absence. Since the relaxant also affected the breathing, air had to be administered through a face mask attached to a large rubber bladder pumped by hand. To keep the air passage open, and to prevent the tongue getting bitten during the convulsions, a stubby black plastic tube, curved and with fat lips, was inserted into the mouth, pinning down the tongue.

The anaesthetic took quick effect. When Geoff was unconscious, three of us held down the blanket covering him, a further restraint to prevent any injury arising from the convulsions.

The doctor looked at Geoff's notes again, then took the electrodes handed to him by the sister. The cloth-covered discs had been moistened in a special electrolyte to enhance electrical contact with the skin. He held them briefly in the air, one in each hand, like someone holding aloft a carving knife and fork before plunging them into the Sunday roast. He rocked slightly on his heels, then slowly bent forward and placed one electrode on each of Geoff's temples. There was a complete, reverential silence. Even the old lady had temporarily ceased her dental lamentations.

He pressed the button at the end of one of the electrodes and there was a brief buzz like a distant doorbell.

Geoff began convulsing. The doctor handed the electrodes back to the sister and watched dispassionately as Geoff's face twitched and his legs gave repeated little kicks. We kept a tight hold on the blanket. "Must have been hell in the old days before they used relaxants," observed one of the other nurses on blanket-restraint duty. "When they did straight ECT. I read that patients would sometimes bang about so much when they convulsed that they'd break an arm or a leg."

"That doesn't happen these days," said the doctor sharply. "We're civilised now."

Geoff continued convulsing for several seconds, then after a series of shudders he became still.

"That's satisfactory," said the doctor, as the sister stepped forward to adjust the mask over Geoff's mouth and rhythmically squeeze the bladder. When she was satisfied he was breathing normally, she stepped back and told us to continue. This meant turning Geoff onto his side. We pushed our arms beneath his bulk, and with one of the others supporting his head we heaved him over and arranged his legs to prevent his rolling onto his back again. I gave the mouthpiece an experimental tug, but it was still clamped tightly between his teeth.

"There was that thing a few years ago," the same nurse said, "when a hospital did ECT for a year or so with a new machine before discovering that it didn't work. It hadn't broken – it couldn't have worked from the start. Wrong wiring or something. But nobody had noticed, and they went on giving shocks which weren't shocks at all. A study then showed that just as many patients improved having these non-shocks as had been getting better when they got real shocks."

"How many was that, then?" asked one of the others.

"I don't remember."

"I can't believe that. You can't tell me that no one noticed the patients weren't convulsing."

"Maybe they thought they were using exactly the right amount of relaxant?"

"More likely the patients were responding to the buzz, going into a fit because of it. You know, conditioned response."

"Pavlov's depressives?" another nurse laughed.

"We haven't got all day," said the doctor, who'd finished checking the next patient's notes. "There's six more to do."

The next patient was another man, a few years older than Geoff. He had a pale face, with tufts of hair sprouting from the skin just below his eyes. He was lying rigidly on his bed, arms stiff by his sides, legs stretched to their limit, feet together and pointing vertically.

"How are you, Mr Peterson?" the doctor asked. "A long time since we last met."

Mr Peterson gave a long groan.

The doctor nodded his head, evidently a trained interpreter of cryptogrammic groans. "We'll soon have you to rights," he assured Mr Peterson, who responded with another long groan.

The procedure for Mr Peterson was the same as for Geoff, then it was repeated for the other five patients. Injection. Electrodes. Buzz. Twitch and jerk. Stillness. Face mask. Roll over. One, two, three, four, five, six, seven. And all the time keeping an eye on those who had received the treatment, to ensure they were still breathing.

By the time the last patient had been rolled over onto her side, Geoff was beginning to stir. I was able to remove the plastic tube from his mouth and drop it into a bowl on the trolley.

"How are you feeling?" I asked.

Geoff looked at me groggily, then closed his eyes again. A few minutes later he reopened them. "When's he going to start?"

"You've had it. All over. Done."

"I don't remember."

"It's all done."

"Was it all right? Did I jerk a lot?"

"A bit. You were fine. Keep lying down for the time being. Don't get up in a hurry. Tea and biscuits as usual when you're ready."

A few minutes later Geoff threw aside the blanket covering him and sat up. "Got me specs? Thanks. Give us me shoes, could you?"

He pulled on his shoes and stood up, supporting himself on the bed rail.

"All right?" I asked.

"Yeah, I think so. Funny, isn't it? I don't remember it."

While Geoff and the other patients were having their tea and biscuits, as though they had just been giving blood, the ward had to be returned to its former state. The oxygen cylinders, which had been standing by in case anyone's breathing became erratic, were trundled back to a side room, unused. The extra blankets were removed from the beds, the incontinence sheets thrown away, the mouthpieces left to soak in a sterilising solution, and the trolley with electrical paraphernalia was pushed into a back room. I washed my hands in a little basin and dried them on the rough, green paper towels with their water-repellent property.

"I'm ready now," said Geoff.

"Have you got your jacket?"

"Where is it?"

"Over that chair."

"Mustn't forget that, must I? You got me notes?"

The doctor had finished writing up the notes in the sister's office. I collected Geoff's and we set off back to the ward.

Turning into one corridor, Geoff stopped and looked around, puzzled.

"This ain't the way," he said.

"Maybe it's not the quickest way," I said. "I still haven't worked out the geography of this place."

"But ECT's that way." He pointed back down the corridor.

"You've already been, Geoff. We're on our way back to our ward."

"Oh yeah." Still looking puzzled, he resumed walking.

It was pigs, I remembered. Some fellow in the nineteenth century had got the idea about inducing fits with electricity to the brain having watched pigs being stunned with electric currents in a slaughterhouse. He'd noticed that they had fits if the current wasn't sufficient to stun them first. Of course, it didn't matter what happened to the pigs' brains as a result; they weren't going to have any further use for them.

"I still don't remember," Geoff said as we neared our ward. "It's funny what it does to you, ain't it?"

"Hilarious," I said, getting out my pass key.

Geoff looked at me strangely.

Dispatches from a Hospital Ward

Introduction

Some while ago I was admitted to hospital at short notice. After a battery of tests, I was wheeled to a bed in the Acute Medical Unit, where I stayed for about thirty hours for further assessment before being moved to the respiratory ward. While on the AMU, I sent my wife a series of emails which, with the personal sections deleted, form the basis of the following.

Saturday 17.43

It's a small ward with six beds. I am in the middle one of three beds against one wall; the other three beds, with the windows behind them, are directly opposite.

A middle-aged, hairy-chested man in the bed diagonally opposite to the left is evidently in training for the Sputum Olympics. He's currently achieving an impressive volume, both in terms of quantity and decibel level; but I reckon he could be in danger of peaking too soon. At the same time, a nurse attending to the patient on my immediate left has just announced that "I need to look at the boil on your bottom." A spot check, I suppose.

The patient whose bed is directly opposite me, currently concealed behind curtains, perhaps doesn't realise that the curtains are acoustically transparent, as, by the sound of it, he is patriotically attempting to fart the National Anthem. He misfires on the line 'Send her victorious' and has another go, but with no greater success. A passing nurse is obliged to suppress – not entirely successfully – unprofessional giggles.

Oh, and now Sputum Man, in between gobs, has taken to demanding that a nurse lop off a problematic toenail, despite being apprised by word and gesture that such a procedure falls outside both her remit and her pay grade. He's far from convinced and repeats his demand for instant toenail-ectomy, while she repeats her disinclination to wield the clippers. Boil-on-the-Bottom Man is wisely keeping quiet.

How unlike the home life of our own dear Queen.

Saturday 19.50

Regrettably, Farting Man has been moved on: tomorrow being Sunday, I had been looking forward to hearing an attempted rendition of 'Oh God, Our Help in Ages Past' – though he would probably have been unable to get past the first two words, albeit repeatedly, resulting in the anguished cry from the nether regions of: "Oh God! Oh God! Oh God!"

In his place is a younger man with very short hair and a glower on his face. I saw him earlier being trundled along the corridors on a mobile bed. Easy to identify as he has an escort of two police officers, who are now sitting on chairs at the foot of his bed, ready to switch off their mobile phones at a moment's notice if they need to spring into action. They don't appear to be armed, though one of them possibly has a taser concealed in his pocket – unless, of course, he's just pleased to see me. The newcomer sits in his chair immediately opposite, staring. Simply staring. In my direction. I bet he's after my flapjack. He's probably Mad Jack Flap, the notorious purloiner of oat-and-syrup-based comestibles.

Confused Man, an elderly chap, has entered the drama. He's in the bed diagonally opposite me to the right. He has been repeatedly trying to get out of bed to go home, despite being linked to a drip and wearing a somewhat inadequate nightshirt. He now believes one of the nurses is his wife and insists that she comes to bed with him. She patiently points out that it's not her bed but his, and he needs to get back into it, but she, according to him, is "very naughty". Hmm.

And now the nurse is warning Confused Man that if he keeps wriggling he'll fall out of bed... Ah, she and a colleague have managed to outmanoeuvre him by putting up the sides of the bed, with Confused Man on the inside and the nurses on the outside in the traditional arrangement. It is 19.57, and the first nurse tells him it's time to get some sleep. An understandable attempt on her part, but I think hope is triumphing over reality – especially as he is now telling her that the police are there to arrest her for putting cream on his legs.

Meanwhile, I had been getting annoyed at the repeated loud pinging noise occurring near me and wondering why someone didn't bloody well deal with it, then a nurse came and revealed that the pinging was coming from my drip because I was sitting in my chair in such a way that my elbow had squashed the feed line.

Hullo – the replacement team of officers guarding Mad Jack Flap has arrived just in time to take the tea trolley into custody and impound a haul of digestive biscuits (or possibly custody creams).

Sunday 06.39

I can't say I had a good night's sleep, but not too bad, I suppose, considering the beeps, strange cries and clanks that punctuated it. The police officers guarding Mad Jack Flap look knackered, and Jack himself is clearly a totally unenterprising malefactor: why no knotting together of sheets to escape through the window? Why no dressing up as a female nurse and sneaking out with the others at the end of a shift? What's wrong with the modern criminal? No get up and go, but lie back and stay... Maybe, like me, he's longing for a cuppa.

Sputum Man made a valiant effort in the night to maintain his output, but he had peaked too soon and, presumably with the aid of the prescribed dose of sleeping tablets in his medicine pot, he sank into a slumber, which was only occasionally broken by the necessity of his making a sound no reasonably sane person would use as the ringtone for their mobile phone. I suspect he is Charles Dickens, rewriting *Great Expectorations*.

Sunday 12.07

I come back from a toilet visit to find that Mad Jack Flap, notorious purloiner of oat-and-syrup-based confection, has either been escorted from the premises by our boys and girls in blue or has finally knotted together his hospital property sheets and descended to the outside world, having locked the local constabulary in the meds cupboard. He failed to get his hands on my supply of flapjack, mainly because I've eaten it all.

We have, however, now acquired Hard-of-Hearing Man to my right, who has informed everyone several times that he hasn't got the charger for his hearing aid and can't hear anything. This explains why I overheard the consultant on his rounds ask him, "Can you read this?" – which struck me as odd on a ward not dealing with eye problems, before I realised the consultant was attempting to consult by means of the written word. Unfortunately, Hard-of-Hearing Man couldn't hear the consultant ask "Can you read this?" so the consultation proved to be terminally useless.

Confused Man continues to pose problems for the staff as he insists on trying to clamber over the bed rail, principally, it would seem, in order to fall over. Just now a willowy nurse did well to catch him in a semi-recumbent position. Said nurse and colleague are, right now, getting him a commode, which has led to the classic exchange:

Nurse 1: I've found a commode.

Nurse 2: Is there anything in it?

Nurse 1: Yes, it's full of wee.

Nurse 2: Best place for it.

Confused Man, appropriately for a Sunday, has just uttered the cry, "Oh, for Christ's sake!" but as this was not the conclusion to a series of intercessory prayers, I'm not sure of its theological or spiritual standing.

Sunday 21.01

New to the ward is Dangly Bits Man. In his eighties, I'd say, he is now the occupant of the bed directly opposite mine, vacated by Mad Jack Flap. Only most of the time he doesn't actually occupy the bed itself but the chair beside it. He wears a permanent facial expression like that of Private Godfrey in *Dad's Army*, namely one of benevolent bewilderment, as well as a fetching off-the-shoulder surgical gown striped like an old-fashioned ice-cream parlour awning. He sits with his legs perpetually spread apart, and he doesn't believe in underwear. Every time I look up from my book, I am confronted at no great distance by that with which I do not wish to be confronted. Certainly not that as displayed by a male octogenarian. This ward may well be the Acute Medical Unit, but his particular medical unit is far from cute and its close visual proximity puts me in constant danger of a relapse.

Also new to the ward, displacing Boil-on-the-Bottom Man, is Indiana Jones Man. A little, elderly fellow, he sports on his leathery head a splendid leathery hat with a circular leathery brim, and in place of a bullwhip he carries no ordinary walking stick but what is probably a sacred relic acquired under dubious circumstances from a South American tribe, or possibly a fertility symbol carved from the horn of a narwhal by the Inuit, or perhaps it's a reduced price end-of-the-line lump of plastic kitsch from Argos. He is, I have been informed, a judo black belt, and as he prowls up and down the ward in his thick leathery boots and a pair of motorcycle goggles, or as, still behatted, he slumbers in his chair like a Mexican at midday, his very leathery presence is a combative challenge to all the forces of sickness and ill health which humanity is heir to. Veritably Indiana Jones and the Last Disease...

Earlier, Son of Hard-of-Hearing Man arrived, summoned by the staff to act as go-between. He loudly informed his father that he's brought in his hearing aid charger, to which HoH Man responded, "I can't hear what you're saying – I haven't got the charger for my hearing aid." This resulted in son, nurses, consultants, porter, ward cleaner, tea lady and all remaining sentient patients chorusing in unison, "We know that!" (All, that is, except for Sputum Man, whose contribution was a long drawn-out deposit of copious gobbing. He appears to be back in training.) Father and son then engaged in a highly public discussion about family members and their failings ("Your mother is a liar, and she steals things"). There is no TV on this ward. Who needs one?

Monday 07.10
Oh well, I've had to take my leave of Sputum Man, Hard-of-Hearing Man, Indiana Jones Man, Dangly Bits Man, Confused Man, and the ghosts of Farting Man, Boil-on-the-Bottom Man and Mad Jack Flap, as late last night I was relocated to a side room on another ward. I wonder what designation I might have been given by my former ward mates. Smug Git Man? Needs-a-Haircut Man? Answers on a postcard, please...

Ah – a cup of tea is on its way. I will sign off.

With grateful thanks to all the staff at the Royal Devon and Exeter Hospital for their fantastic expertise, care and endless patience (and patients).

Deprived Children

The football was worse than Peter had feared. He had on a pair of borrowed boots which were at least a size too large, and the ground was muddy. He ran up and down leaden-footedly, his mind churning over what he would be doing if he weren't there and how he could escape without losing face. His skill with football had always been on the low side; now, with complete lethargy dominant, his ineptitude was embarrassing. It didn't help – quite the opposite – that the kids were football crazy. The entire country was football crazy. It was 1966, with everyone still bathing in the afterglow of England winning the World Cup just a week previously. Was he the only person who loathed the game?

He aimed a kick at the ball and missed, and all the kids fell about laughing. When, a few minutes later, exactly the same thing happened again, his misery deepened.

"Shift yourself, you miserable sod," said Ben, who was refereeing the game. "Kick the thing."

Rousing himself, Peter tried to concentrate for the next few minutes. "Over here!" he cried out. To his dismay, the boy in possession of the ball booted it roughly in his direction. He ran to intercept it. Just before he reached it, an agonising pain shot through his ankle and something hit the back of his knees. He fell to the ground as his nine-year-old opponent charged onto the ball and rapidly dribbled it away.

"Foul!" shouted Peter angrily.

"Piss off!" the nine-year-old shouted back at him.

"Play on," cried Ben.

"Did you see what that little swine did?" Peter said to Alison at half-time.

She had turned up to dispense drinks and biscuits.

"They are not little swine," reproved Alison. "They're 'deprived children'." She put the expression – as, Peter had noticed, everyone else did – in audible speech marks.

"All right," Peter said. "Did you see what that little 'deprived child' did? Hacked my ankle. God, it hurts."

"Which one?"

"The left one. It's gonna be a mass of bruises."

"Which *child*? I'm not interested in your ankle."

Peter looked around and identified his attacker.

"That's Ronnie," said Alison. "I gather he models himself on Nobby Stiles. He's one of your four. You're supposed to be developing a supportive relationship with him. He's from a very deprived family."

"I'll deprive him of his bollocks if he does that to me again," Peter muttered to himself.

It was Monday, the first day of the holiday scheme for 'deprived children' in a depressed area of East London. On his arrival on Saturday evening at Beauchamp House, which would be his base for the next fortnight, Peter had been given a green folder with his name and the legend 'holiday scheme' neatly written on it. Inside the folder were a provisional programme for the fortnight, a map of the area, bus routes, a sheet of paper headed 'useful telephone numbers', and a list of children's names. Some of the names were marked with an asterisk; these were the ones allocated to him, the ones he had to 'develop a supportive relationship with'.

Since then, the misgivings which had been rattling around inside his head had, like alien seed pods, suddenly bursting forth with virulent growth, burgeoned into frantic boredom. The enthusiasm and commitment of the other volunteers depressed him. How could they enjoy – actually *enjoy* – spending a fortnight in the company of a vast horde of unruly, demanding kids, 'deprived' or not?

On Thursday the weather let them down and for the entire morning it streamed with rain. All the activities had to take place in the large hall that doubled up as a gym. The noise was terrific. Games were organised which needed excruciatingly high energy levels. There was a game of Hunt the Tiger, with Peter as the tiger. A precarious pathway had been constructed around the hall out of orange boxes, planks, ropes, wall bars, tables, chairs and vaulting horses. He had to leap from item to item, with his feet not touching the floor at any stage, while the children charged after him. Fear spurred him on – fear of being caught by the wild, shouting, cheering, ghastly pack of bloodthirsty little swine. *Lord of the Flies* stuff. Oblivious to the stiffness in his ankle, he raced around the circuit, but halfway round for the second time he tripped and fell. The children swarmed over him, shouting out in their glee at capturing him. Peter lay dazed on the floor, swearing silently.

On Saturday afternoon, when Peter limped back to the centre following another game of football, he found Alison talking to a newcomer.

"This is Peter," Alison said. "It's his first time here as well. Peter, this is Barbara."

Peter nodded curtly at Barbara, who responded with a very slight inclination of the head while gazing steadily at him. As she and Alison continued their conversation, Peter slumped down into a chair and closed his eyes. The arrival of another do-gooder. Oh God. Another week of this would drive him crazy. He'd clocked up a good number of points on the credit side of life's ledger; now he needed to find a justifiable excuse for leaving. Death of a relative? Contracting a deadly disease? Outbreak of World War Three? Rather extreme measures, and not easy to engineer.

Alison went out of the room. There was a long silence. Forgetting that he was not alone, Peter groaned out loud, and was startled when a voice spoke.

"You sound tired," Barbara had said. She sounded amused.

Peter opened one eye. "I am," he grunted.

"What have you been doing today?"

"Surviving."

"As bad as that, is it?" To the amusement was added a faint concern.

Peter opened both eyes. "Oh, it's well worth it," he said insincerely.

Barbara tilted her head slightly to one side and looked at Peter quizzically. "Mmm," she said, adding, "when do they have supper here?"

There were no activities planned for the next day, Sunday. Peter stayed in his sleeping bag until gone ten, then hunger forced him up. No one else was around. He went to buy a paper, and was reading it while eating toast when Barbara appeared. She had a very relaxed way of moving which affected Peter strongly; it gave him the impression that she could, if she chose, move from one place to another without disturbing the air in-between.

"Can I?" She picked up one of the sections of the paper and sat down at the table. "Where are the others?"

"Dunno," said Peter. "Out somewhere."

"Together?"

"Again, dunno."

"What are you doing today?"

"At the risk of sounding monotonous, dunno. Lounge around, I suppose. I did think of going back home, but it's a bit of a distance. What are you doing today?"

"Dunno," said Barbara, mimicking Peter's tone then laughing, but without malice. "But I'm not going to stay around here all day. It'll bore me to tears. Let's go out."

"Where?"

"Anywhere."

Peter nodded. "You're on," he said in delight.

They caught the Tube to the city centre. Over a pub lunch they talked at length. Barbara, it turned out, had graduated from art college a year previously, and was now scraping a living by teaching at adult education classes and doing bar work to fund her art.

"How come you're doing this holiday scheme thing?" he asked.

"Alison asked if I could," Barbara said. "We've known each other for years. She's a good sort, much more altruistic than I am, and I felt it was about time to do something. Actually," she laughed, "the real reason is she's been nagging me for ages to lend a hand, and I finally capitulated – only way to stop her nagging! And you? Why're you doing it?"

Peter shrugged. "Beauchamp House is owned by my college. Beauchamp College. They oversee a whole load of community projects, and the college dean hinted pretty heavily I ought to put in a stint. It's not really my scene, though."

"I'd gathered that! What is your scene, then?"

So he told her about the music he liked, the band he played with, the English degree course he was part way through, his enjoyment of cycling. And she told him about her painting and sculpting. She told him about the intermingling of doubts and certainties when she was engaged on a work, and the interweaving of richly productive periods with long spells of inertia. She told him of the exhaustion on completing a work, and the terror on starting a new one. She described with her fingers the lines of a wind-felled tree she had seen and was seeking to reproduce; her voice conveyed what at first Peter privately labelled as overenthusiasm, but as she continued, it became clear that her commitment went far deeper than mere enthusiasm. The word 'passion' came to mind. She conveyed a passion which amazed and fascinated him.

"Come on, I'll take you around the Tate," she said when he confessed that his knowledge of art was minimal. He acquiesced despite an initial twinge of doubt, but it was no witless gallop through the rooms Barbara had in mind. They looked at only a dozen or so paintings. She made brief remarks, single words or short phrases, a command directing his attention to a tiny detail or recurring motif, a question which in the very asking made him look afresh. Suddenly, in her presence, Peter was made aware of dimensions he had never dreamed existed. Her eyes opened his eyes to colour and shape, pattern and balance, and he began to see the paintings in a way totally new to him. He was astounded by the depth and spread of feeling, life and love that were portrayed.

"It's the way you see, not what you see," said Barbara.

It had never before entered his mind that such creations had a life and a dynamism which could evoke echoes in himself, and yet here, as they looked at them with intense purpose, the interaction between the paintings, himself and the catalytic passion of the woman beside him sent shock waves through him. He dimly realised he was undergoing an initiation into realms he had had no conception of previously, and he longed to immerse himself fully in this new universe.

One evening they were in the pub sitting slightly apart from the others. Barbara asked what his plans were when he completed his university course.

"Dunno," said Peter. It had become their catchphrase. "All I do know is that I won't go into teaching."

"What is there that's really important to you?" Barbara demanded.

"Really important?"

"Mmm," Barbara frowned. Her narrow eyebrows were drawn close together, as though the intensity of her look were to be discharged in a series of fierce electric sparks between them. "Is there anything which really makes you say, 'This is absolutely central to me? This is what I *have* to be involved in?' Not 'this is what I would like to be involved with, this is what I think I might like to do' but 'this is what I *must* do'?"

"What sort of thing do you mean?" Peter asked.

"Something that gives shape and structure and meaning to your life.

Something which you really get to grips with – or rather, something which really gets to grips with you. It's that way round."

Peter pondered. "Dunno! I mean, it's not easy to say. Why do you think it's important?"

"I think it's important because it *is* important. I think we need a central something to our lives if we're going to be properly human, not just sort of blobs of sentient protoplasm." She began to look sad, and her eyes took on the look of focusing on internal images. "So many people seem to be without something central to their lives, a core which gives meaning, raises you into being human. Does that make sense? So many people are without that core. They fill their time, but that's all. There isn't a central, organising principle to their lives. They live jellyfish lives. Blob lives. Eat, sleep and fuck lives. Nothing more."

"Sounds pretty good to me," said Peter with a laugh.

"You're not a blob," said Barbara. "At least, I don't think you are."

"So what is it for you? What's important for you? Your painting, I suppose?"

"Oh yes! I don't regard my art as just an activity I happen to like, something which keeps me out of mischief until I die. It actually *is* my life. And it's about – well, about real connections – it's about reality. It *is* reality for me. We all need our windows onto reality, our doors into it, and painting and sculpting are my doors and windows. I think I see you as someone who's waiting to find his window. That sounds a daft way to put it, but it's the best I can do. I just want to say, don't be prepared to accept second best. Be willing to risk the best. When you suddenly realise that you're saying 'I'm willing to risk total failure for the sake of this' – whatever 'this' might be – well, that's a clear sign, in my opinion. It's not 'what can I succeed at?' that's the criterion but 'what to me is so important that I am willing to risk total failure on its behalf?'"

"It's true enough that there's nothing like that for me," Peter admitted. "There are a number of things I find interesting, but nothing that I'd say is of all-consuming importance. Certainly nothing that I want to say I'd want to risk failing at."

"Not your music?"

"Not really," Peter shook his head slowly. "I mean, I love playing with the other guys – we have a laugh and we also play some good stuff. But it's not what you're meaning."

That conversation with Barbara left Peter feeling strangely troubled. Her words touched on elements which, now she *had* touched on them, he knew to be crucial, although before she'd spoken he'd had no inkling of consciousness about them. What was important to him? What was of literally vital importance? It was as though he had been living in a walled garden and had not even seen the walls until someone – Barbara – began opening the doors. Only then did the existence of the walls become apparent, and his universe suddenly felt very circumscribed, death-dealing. The possibility of moving out beyond the walls struck him with great force, bringing with it both excitement and anxiety.

Peter now simultaneously longed for the end of the week and dreaded it with equal fervency. To be shot of the kids would be wonderful, but it would also mean the end of being in Barbara's presence. Practicalities of seeing her again, the sooner the better, had to be arranged. He knew that she would be off to Cornwall for a week to stay with some cousins, and then back to the house in Greenwich she shared with others. Peter himself had no definite plans for the rest of the summer.

Friday arrived, the last day of the holiday scheme. In the morning, Alison, Peter, Barbara and another volunteer called Roger took a large group of children to a park, which contained an adventure playground and an animal sanctuary. Alison and Roger took one group off to the animals, while Peter and Barbara were in charge of the smaller adventure playground contingent.

"Look! Swings!" said Barbara as the children charged off. "Let's have a go on the swings! I haven't been on a swing for years!"

She ran across to them. The frame was exceptionally tall.

"Come on!" she shouted imperiously, settling in one. "Come and give me a push!"

He followed her to the swings. "Hang on tight!"

"Not too high!" she squealed, suddenly girlish, as he pushed her hard.

"Too late!" said Peter. He felt intensely happy to have a legitimate reason for touching Barbara. His hand moved back and forth in time with the rhythm of her swinging; and on each downswing, as he placed his hand on the small of her back and thrust her skyward again, a thrill shot through his body. He pushed her more vigorously, and she cried out.

"This is wonderful!" she shouted. "Harder! Push me harder!"

Her arty skirt began billowing out. She swept up into the sky until the chains holding the swing were way above the horizontal, then swooped down again and up the other half of the arc. Peter now barely had time to push her, she was moving so fast through the lowest point of the trajectory.

He became mesmerised by the rhythm of her movement. His eyes turned automatically to follow her, as though an invisible thread connected the pupils of his eyes to her body. It seemed that a spotlight was illuminating her with a preternatural light. She was at the centre of a circle of illumination, and beyond the circumference of the circle all was dark, relegated to the realms of non-existence.

She was saying something, calling out something to him. He blinked and shook his head; as he did so, the spotlight was doused and the rest of the universe sprang back into existence.

"No more!" she was crying out. "Let me slow down! No more! Peter, no more!" He wondered why she continued calling out before he realised that his arm was still automatically moving with her rhythm, his hand still pushing her. It took an effort of will to instruct his arm to cease operations. It stayed suspended in mid-air for a moment until Barbara's back struck it. Peter lowered his arm.

As Barbara slowed down, she dragged her feet on the ground to hasten the process until the swing was almost stationary. She half-fell out of it into Peter's arms, deliberately positioned for that possibility.

"It's marvellous," she gasped, laughing. "Go on, you must have a go."

Peter clambered onto the swing and gripped the chains. Abruptly he was way up in the air. Barbara's hand on his back became a wonderful, regular, welcome event. Effortlessly he soared into the sky, down and up again, down and up, rising higher with each oscillation.

"Whay hey!" he shouted. "Wheee!"

Barbara was shouting something. He could not catch her words.

"What?"

"Close your eyes! Try it with your eyes closed!"

Peter closed his eyes. It was an extraordinary sensation; he felt right out of himself. The hand on the small of the back, the upward rush against gravity, a split second of suspension in mid-air caught between the final fragment of upward movement and the downward pull of gravity, then the capitulation to gravity and the acceleration earthwards in maybe a second of free fall.

When he finally slowed down and, like Barbara before him, had half-fallen out of the swing, he leaned on her, feigning greater exhaustion than he felt. Barbara put her arm round him. They were both laughing with great exhilaration.

"Let's go on it together," Barbara said. Again she sounded girlish in her enthusiasm.

"Will it take our weight?"

"Are you saying I'm fat?" Barbara said with mock indignation. She was anything but. "Course it will. They're chains, plenty strong enough. You sit on the seat first. That's right."

With Peter on the swing, Barbara faced him and, hitching up her skirt, tucked it between her legs. Then she grasped one of the chains and clambered awkwardly onto him. The swing bucked and tipped like a protesting horse. Barbara's face was flushed and she was still laughing.

Eventually they were settled, Peter sitting on the swing and Barbara sitting on his lap, facing him, her legs spread either side of him.

"Comfortable?" Peter asked.

"As I'll ever be," laughed Barbara.

"I'm glad one of us is!" said Peter. "Right, let's see if we can actually get this thing to fly. I'll lean forward and you lean back when I say go, and I'll try to kick us off with my feet – but, ouch, it's difficult to move 'em."

The swing started to twist bizarrely, then some semblance of swinging motion began. Peter pushed purposefully against the ground with his feet, an action which automatically pressed him harder against Barbara. Soon they were swinging gently, and the rhythm of their bodies maintained the motion. As they swung, Barbara was fractionally sliding back and forth on his lap, her buttocks and thighs performing a massage on his legs.

He lost awareness of all but the immediate sensations: the weight of Barbara on his lap and her rhythmic swaying, the dreamy look on her face, the feel of her hand pressing into his back as she held onto him, the creaking protests of the overburdened swing. He looked at the curve of her breasts pushing against the pale yellow T-shirt covering them. The rightness of their contours gladdened him.

She started humming, a tuneless hum that rose and fell, creating itself moment by moment. Peter too began to hum, and their two hums intertwined, dying and reviving, sometimes together, sometimes in a form of counterpoint, sometimes low and barely audible, then gathering in strength to the volume almost of a shout before waning again. Then, with no apparent signal between them, they allowed the hums to fade away simultaneously, all the while continuing the gentle swaying which maintained the movement of the swing. Peter's eyes had closed. Being with this glorious woman – was this to be the core, the centre of his life? The thought was overwhelming.

"Mister," said a voice. "Miss. I've banged me knee. Ronnie pushed me off the frame and it hurt me knee."

Peter opened his eyes and looked at the owner of the voice, an eight-year-old girl called Mandy. He regarded her with annoyance. For a short while he had completely forgotten about this lot. But Mandy looked so sorrowful, on the verge of tears, that Peter's annoyance vanished in an instant and he felt sorry for the kid.

He and Barbara extricated themselves from the swing. "Let's have a look," Barbara said. "Oh dear, you have scraped it, haven't you? Does it hurt?"

The little girl nodded, still not crying. "A bit."

"Come on," said Barbara kindly, "let's go and wash it."

"You'll be all right," said Peter. "You're being very brave."

"Ronnie pushed me, mister," said Mandy.

"It might have been an accident," said Peter. "But I'll have a word with him."

As Barbara took Mandy to the ladies', Peter went looking for Ronnie.

That afternoon, the final session of the holiday scheme, there was a party. Traditional children's food was in great abundance. Paper hats were provided for all. Ben demonstrated great skill as a Punch and Judy man. Silly games were played with forfeits.

Peter joined in with moderate enthusiasm. He wore his paper hat without too much embarrassment; laughed at Punch and Judy, shouting out with the children when Mr Punch asked them to; helped dole out the food; and as a forfeit in one of the games he had to mime to a record he privately despised. His mime was so successful he did an encore and received a rousing round of applause.

"'Ere," said one of the older girls, making up to him afterwards, "you're dead fab. You gonna be a pop star?"

Small presents were distributed to the children as parents started to arrive to reclaim their offspring.

"Are you gonna come here again soon?" said the same girl, sounding hopeful, before reluctantly leaving, swinging her hips provocatively.

"You've made a hit there," Barbara murmured in his ear.

"I'd get arrested," Peter murmured in return.

After supper that evening with the other volunteers, Peter packed his bag. Most of the others were staying on until the next morning, but he was leaving that evening, as was Barbara. Packing complete, he knocked on the open door of her room. Barbara was also packing.

"Hi," she said.

"Hi. Barbara, could you let me have your address?"

Barbara paused in the middle of folding a towel. "What for?"

Peter was surprised. "I'd like to keep in contact."

She put the towel in her case and moved over to him. Putting her hand on his arm, she looked at him. A few inches shorter than him, she had to tilt her head back, and her hair, falling away from her face, revealed it in a fashion that made Peter's heart quicken.

She gazed at him for what seemed like several minutes, though it could not have been more than a few seconds, and Peter gazed steadily back. Then she lowered her gaze, moved her hand on his arm in a comforting manner, and looked up at him again. "I really don't think it would be a good idea," she said.

"Why not?"

She worried her top lip with her teeth, a characteristic he had noticed before. "It doesn't feel right."

It was dismay that Peter felt. "What's wrong with keeping in contact? I'd like to."

"So would I, in a way. But it doesn't feel right," she repeated.

"I don't understand."

"I'm not sure I can explain, put it in words." She removed her hand from his arm and took a pace back. "I haven't really enjoyed this week, but I haven't not enjoyed it either," she continued. "The one thing I have totally enjoyed, though, has been your company. It's been lovely to have you around. You've been a sort of ally."

"Yes," said Peter. "I know what you mean. At the end of the first week, before you turned up, I just did not know how I could survive another week of it."

"We helped each other survive."

"But it's been more than that," said Peter.

"Yes and no. I like you a lot," Barbara said earnestly. "An awful lot. But because it's been so good with you, I want to leave it there. To say that the fun bits we've had belong to this last week. If we kept up contact, I'm afraid it would fall to pieces."

She went up to him again and put her hands on his shoulders, then pressed herself against him. Peter hesitated a moment, then put his arms around her and rested his chin gently on top of her head.

Barbara spoke again, her voice muffled. "I want this week that I've known you to be complete in itself, not straggling on. I don't mean I'd hate to see you again – I don't mean that at all. But I want to let it happen if it happens, not force it to happen. After all" —she pulled back slightly, and Peter relaxed his embrace while still keeping his arms round her— "you never know but I might be crazy enough to come here next year if Alison turns on the moral pressure again. And so might you. In a year's time we might both have forgotten how ghastly children are, so we could end up signing on for another period of purgatory!"

Peter felt himself to be at a point of decision. Petulance or gratitude? Could he allow the gratitude for her presence over the past week to obliterate his disappointment at her not wishing to maintain contact? He felt dizzy with the need to respond. Petulance was easier. Annoyance, anger, miserableness – they were all easier than gratitude. He could punish her, try to make her feel guilty at his being hurt. But she had opened up so many things for him in the space of a few days. She had shown him the world through her eyes. Intensity and freedom. Because of her he could never be the same; priorities were shifting, new understandings emerging. He had come along reluctantly, ostensibly to help so-called 'deprived children'. It now felt that all along he had also been deprived, and she, Barbara, had set in motion thoughts and feelings and awarenesses he had never before known, releasing him from his deprivation.

He held her tight, and again with his chin resting on her head he stared through the grimy, curtainless window into the cluttered yard below.

Half an hour later they left together for the station. Barbara refused to allow him to carry her bag.

"Well, it's goodbye then," said Peter, when the time came for them to go their separate ways.

They kissed.

"It's been lovely with you," Barbara said.

"*Will* I see you again?" Peter couldn't stop himself asking.

There was a pause.

"Dunno," Barbara said softly. "But if we never see each other again – well, have a good life!"

He stood and watched as she walked away. She turned and waved, then went through the open barrier onto her platform. Peter headed for his platform, and when on it he looked across to where Barbara should have been waiting for her train. But he could not see her.

The Armadillo Project

George and I arrived at Trevor's lair on Dartmoor early evening. Well, I say 'lair', but it was more an ancient and rambling pile, where the ghosts of gigantic hounds and deer-stalkered detectives doubtless still roamed, luring the unwary traveller into the great Grimpen Mire.

"What have we let ourselves in for?" George muttered as we drew up at the place.

"A touch of *Rocky Horror*?" I suggested.

"I'm not dressed for it."

Neither, thankfully, was Trevor dressed for it, being attired as he was in conventional male clothes. He did, however, look like an escapee from a Gothic novel. In the five or six years that had passed since we'd last seen him, he'd become rather gaunt and wild-eyed, with his thin hair containing curious patches of baldness. Overall, he looked distinctly shambolic.

"Hello, you fellows, good to see you! Thanks for coming," were his opening words. Conventional enough, yes, but thereafter convention went out the window. "Let me show you my laboratory," he continued. Not, you'll notice, 'did you have a good journey?' or 'how about a drink?' or 'let me show you to your rooms'. His laboratory and his great project – 'The Armadillo Project', as George and I had dubbed it years ago – alone occupied his thoughts.

The laboratory was a huge space littered with instruments and devices, such as a batch of computers, oscilloscopes, cameras, printers and the like, but the outstanding feature was a vast, horizontal, metal cylindrical affair – ten or twelve metres long and four or five metres in diameter, with numerous leads snaking from it to a bank of instruments and monitors. There was a metal ladder leading to a hatchway, and a single long glass window occupying the side facing us.

"Flotation tank," Trevor said abruptly. "Isn't she a beauty?"

"If you say so," George said.

"What's it for?" I asked.

"Floating in?" George guessed.

"Sensory deprivation," said Trevor. "This is where it all takes place. This is where I will be *reconstructing reality!*"

Reconstructing reality by the power of thought alone – that was the essence of Trevor's project. And we had been invited to witness its culmination.

The Armadillo Project had its genesis back in our shared school days and the Electronics Society. Now, let's get one thing straight from the start: contrary to received wisdom, the school's Electronics Society was the cunning wheeze of George and myself, not Trevor. That said, I completely agree that without Trevor it could never have come into existence; after all, he was into computers and all things electronic long before they became such a major part of everyone's lives, and I'm talking here about the mid-1960s. As became legendary throughout the school, with the encouragement of the physics master, Horace 'Charged Balls' Occomore, Trevor built his own analogue computer from a whole batch of pieces scavenged from old valve radios and the like, which on its completion became the centrepiece of an open-day exhibition that made the school's reputation for groundbreaking education.

George and I were minor players in this particular success. He had roped us into building the contraption, to help with stripping the valves and condensers and twiddly bits from the weird assortment of electrical junk he had accumulated, and to assist with the soldering and suchlike of his brainchild – though, looking back, I suspect that in reality our involvement was as much to ensure that his progress towards triumph was properly witnessed, as he admitted to be the case at the culmination of his electronic wizardry many years later. But it was during the summer holidays following that triumph that George and I came up with the idea of establishing an Electronics Society, though neither of us had any real competence in that area. What we did have competence in, though, was devising ways to benefit from Trevor's particular genius.

Having persuaded him that this was the ideal way to further his electronic skills and opportunities, George and I put together a package to take to the Head at the beginning of the autumn term. The Head listened, was impressed, and bit. Bit big. Dazzled by Trevor's ability, along with George's and my detailed plans, he authorised the immediate establishment of an Electronics Society, and (as George and I had surmised he would) allocated a considerable sum of money for its operation. We had drawn up, as part of the plans, a highly detailed financial forecast regarding necessary equipment and materials which, supported by 'Charged Balls', was immediately ratified by the Head. We were in business.

A lot of fellow pupils, particularly from the lower forms, joined and enjoyed evenings of mucking about with transistors and soldering irons, while George, Trevor and I got on with the real business as we saw it: namely, using the equipment we'd bought with the allocated funds for Trevor to devise and build miniature radios capable of receiving the pirate pop music radio stations, which George (in charge of finance, and honing his skills in what is now referred to as 'creative accountancy') and I (in charge of below-the-radar marketing) then sold to pupils, both of our school and of other schools we had contact with – the local girls' school in particular, where the gorgeous Beth as head girl had immense influence. The radios were fantastic little devices, easy to conceal and listen to through an earpiece during tedious lessons, and they sold like the proverbial hot cakes. In the autumn term and the following spring term we made a mint of money, split four ways (Beth included).

Then it all went tits up. How the staff discovered our spin-off activities we never learned, but George and I were hauled up before the Head and ruthlessly cross-examined. Unwilling to become grasses, we managed to keep Trevor out of the firing line, insisting that we were the culprits for taking advantage of him – an easy enough task considering his unworldliness. We were lucky to avoid being expelled; probably what saved us was George and me being university material, and the Head being obsessed with maximising the number of university places offered to pupils of our school. We were, however, stripped of our status as prefects, had removed from us all the privileges usually given to sixth-formers, and were generally held to be in eternal disgrace.

Those repercussions didn't really bother us too much, but what did rankle was that Trevor, with his computer, had been entered by the school in some national 'Young Inventor of the Year' competition, which he only went and won, along with substantial prize money which he failed to share; and then the school gave him a special award for initiative and enterprise, and a scholarship to support him through university. No mention of George and me, even though without us he wouldn't have got anywhere. Yes, I admit it, it rankled…

After university, George and I kept in regular contact as we pursued our respective careers in accountancy and teaching, but both of us lost touch with Trevor. At some stage I heard from another old school friend that Trevor was pursuing a stellar career with some electronics company, and then later, in the mid-nineties, George picked up something in the press about Trevor Baring being 'a name to watch' in the rapidly expanding field of information technology. But neither of us had any direct contact with him for literally decades.

It came as a surprise, then, to get a message from him a few years ago through the now defunct Friends Reunited networking website. *Hi Paul! Remember me?* his message went. *Electronics whizz-kid! Still whizzing! Thought it would be good to get back in contact – maybe meet up sometime? And are you still in contact with George?*

I had joined Friends Reunited to try to track down Beth, my marriage having recently gone pear-shaped, and, frankly, being contacted by Trevor the nerd was poor compensation for having failed to track down Beth the beauty. But, more out of boredom than real interest, I rang George to get his view.

"What do you reckon?" I said, having read him the message. "Do you want to meet up with the little turd?"

"Harsh words, Paul," he said, adding, "Harsh but fair. Still, let bygones be bygones, eh? Whatever a bygone is."

The upshot was that, three or four weeks later, George and I were sitting in a pub just down the road from our old school, listening to Trevor in full flow. He was doing all right for himself in some independent business he had set up, inventing and developing a whole range of electronic devices: anything from archaeological tools for detecting buried remains to zoological gadgets for monitoring migrating animals.

"But what I'm working on currently," he said, as George set up the second round, "is the most exciting! Absolutely revolutionary! A synthesis of philosophy, psychology, biology and electronics!"

"And accountancy?" asked George.

"Tell us about it," I said.

He needed no encouraging. "I'm developing a biofeedback machine which will give its user the power to change reality simply by thinking about it! Or rather" —he leaned forward and lowered his voice dramatically— "by *not* thinking about it."

"In what way 'change reality'?" I said cautiously.

"The basic premise," he continued in the kind of voice reserved for instructing particularly dim infants, "is that reality is an infinitely malleable construct of the mind-brain, not a fixed state of objectivity."

"That's pretty obvious." I injected heavy sarcasm into my voice. "Wouldn't you say so, George? Pretty damned elementary."

"What I'd say is that someone hasn't been taking their medication," George offered.

"And if you *don't* think about it hard enough," Trevor said, ignoring our comments, "you can change reality into whatever you want it to be."

This was eye-wateringly bonkers. "Are you saying," I said facetiously, "that if I think about it hard enough—"

"Or don't think about it!" George interjected.

"—then I could change this pint of beer into, say, an armadillo?"

Trevor waved his hand impatiently in the way that he had, nearly knocking over the armadillo-in-waiting. "I'm being serious," he said crossly. "This is a serious philosophical theory with major practical consequences. But if you fellows can't be bothered to make use of what you laughingly refer to as your minds, then so be it. All I can say is—"

"Peace! Peace! We're all agog," George soothed him. "Whatever a 'gog' is. Carry on, Trev."

Having looked quizzically at both of us, and presumably deciding that we were, despite appearances, genuinely interested, Trevor relaxed again.

"Well," he said, "what I'm interested in doing is applying biofeedback to the brain's perceptual constructive activity. You know what biofeedback is?"

"Isn't that what I give my tomato plants?" George asked as I shook my head.

Trevor sighed. "Founder members of the Electronics Society and you don't know what biofeedback is. In simple terms, biofeedback is a method of training a person to acquire control over various happenings in his body which are not normally under conscious control. A lot of things that happen with your body take place automatically, don't they? The rate at which your hair grows or your food is digested and so on. They just happen. They're not under the control of your will in the same way that, say, raising your arm is."

"Good idea," said George, and raised his arm, complete with pint of beer in hand, and took a long draught.

"Precisely," said Trevor. "You want to lift your arm, so you lift your arm. You have control over it."

"Unless he's completely blotto at the time!" I laughed.

"Pre*cise*ly!" Trevor repeated. "It takes something like excess alcohol or a broken bone to *stop* you having that control, to break the link between your will and your action. But as far as something like, say, blood pressure is concerned, there isn't such a direct link. However – and this is the crucial bit – by biofeedback mechanisms a person can learn to alter his blood pressure at will. It's well attested."

He explained. Briefly, the idea is that you rig up a machine which measures your blood pressure and converts it into a continuous audible sound. The higher your blood pressure, the higher the pitch of the note emitted; the lower your blood pressure, the lower the note. The sound fluctuates anyway because of ordinary fluctuations in your blood pressure, and so, for example, to lower your blood pressure you have to listen to the note being emitted and concentrate on making the pitch go lower. You don't know what your body's doing to make the blood pressure go down, but because you've got the audible feedback from the machine you apparently learn unconsciously how to do it. It sounded weird, but Trevor assured us that it had been demonstrated time and again under the strictest laboratory conditions.

"Now, my idea," he continued, "is that this same technique could be used to train a person to gain control over the brain's perceptual constructive activity. What I'm talking about" —he again leaned forward and lowered his voice— "is *the reordering of reality*! For example, take this glass of beer—"

"You mean, this armadillo," said George.

"It doesn't actually exist – or rather, it doesn't exist in the way we think it exists. You see, we don't actually experience the glass of beer in itself, do we? By definition, we experience experiences, and what we think of as objective reality is in fact only the end product of the brain's perceptual constructive activity."

"That," I pointed out, "is the third time you've used that phrase, and I still haven't got a clue what it means."

"All right," said Trevor, "let me ask you this: what does the brain actually *do*? I'll tell you. The brain receives a load of data from our various senses – vision and hearing and touch and so forth – and then it takes all this data and fits it together into a coherent whole. It makes patterns, forms causal links and so on. I'm putting all this very simplistically, of course, so you fellows can follow it."

"Jolly decent of you, old boy," I said.

"And the end result of all that fitting together is what we call objective reality – and that fitting together process itself is what I call the brain's perceptual constructive activity."

He went on to compare the brain's activity with building a boat. The argument went roughly as follows: in order to build a boat, you need wood and rope and metal and glue and rivets and canvas and varnish and a whole load of other raw materials. But you also need a set of instructions for fitting the raw materials together to create the boat. But suppose you assemble the wood and rope and metal and so on a different way, according to a different set of instructions; then you get perhaps another type of boat, or perhaps something totally different altogether, like a gazebo or a scale model of Westminster Palace or a winning entry for the Turner Prize.

"Now," he said, "suppose you could train the brain to apply a *different* set of instructions of how to put together all the sensory data it receives? Same sensory data coming in but different building instructions applied to it! What would you get?"

"An armadillo," George insisted firmly.

"You get *an alternative reality*! You could learn to change reality to whatever you choose. Simply by changing the brain's—"

"Perceptual constructive activity!" George and I beat him to it.

"Exactly! Well done, you fellows, maybe you're not as thick as I was beginning to think."

"Perhaps we've managed to change *your* brain's perceptual constructive activity," said George.

"Hmm," said Trevor.

"But how do you train the brain to do that?" I asked.

"That's where the biofeedback comes into its own. I intend to use biofeedback techniques to gain conscious control over my brain's perceptual constructive activity. Once you have that control, there's an infinite number of realities you could choose to construct."

He fell silent, offering no further explanations, which was just as well as my brain's perceptual constructive activity was beginning to seize up. George, however, was still master of the situation. He tapped my empty glass.

"Fancy another armadillo?" he asked.

George and I continued to meet regularly over the next few years. At first Trevor and his 'Armadillo Project', as we mockingly dubbed it, featured in our pub conversations, but it soon dropped off the agenda. Neither George nor I received responses from Trevor to emails we sent him, so we eventually gave up on him and his weird notions. Besides, other things were taking our attention: I had finally tracked down the gorgeous Beth only to discover she was living with a certain Miranda, so I was now pursuing the recently divorced head of history at the school where I taught; and George had jacked in accountancy in order to head up some financial advice service specialising in offshore investments.

It was about five years later that Trevor popped up again, sending George and me the same email: *How are you fellows? If you remember my biofeedback project, it's just about ready to have the first major run. As fellow founder members of the Electronics Society, you should be here for it! Can you come? I'd v much appreciate it.* He added a number of possible dates for us to go down to Devon, where he had been lurking ever since going solo.

"Well?" I said to George. "Shall we visit the turdette?"

"You still haven't forgiven him, have you?" said George.

"Have you?"

"Not so as you'd notice," he admitted.

So we agreed to go, and fixed a date with Trevor.

There we were, then, George and I, in Trevor's Dartmoor lair, wondering what the hell we had let ourselves in for.

Over the evening meal – spartan, vegetarian, no alcohol – Trevor brought us up to date with his thinking. As far as I could gather, he had refined his concept of the 'perceptual constructive activity' of the brain by now referring to two distinct activities: what he called the brain's 'receptive' activity and its 'constructive' activity. "By the 'receptive activity'," he explained, "I mean what the brain does in simply receiving and acknowledging sensory data, whereas the 'constructive activity' is what the brain does with the sensory data in creating our perception of reality."

George and I nodded as though wisely, but with little comprehension. I found myself expecting a massive thunderstorm to break out over Dartmoor, or at least over the house, with tremendous lightning flashes which would power whatever madness Trevor intended pursuing.

"I've been trying out a whole range of biofeedback techniques," he said, topping up our glasses of pomegranate and asparagus juice. "And I finally identified the one which enables me to monitor these activities separately. I can now use biofeedback to enter a state of consciousness in which my brain receives sensory data *but does not construct a reality from it*. How about that, you fellows?"

"I wish my brain didn't construct a real taste from this stuff," said George, swirling round the alcohol-free muck.

"The trouble is, though," Trevor continued, "I've run into a paradox. I'd seen it looming for some while, and I've now reached the point where I have to resolve it if I'm to make the final leap."

He then fell silent and entered some form of reverie. I wondered if his brain's receptive activity had closed down prematurely. George shrugged.

"Okay, what's this paradox, then?" I asked eventually. "Trev, what's the paradox?"

"The paradox?" He came out of his reverie with a start. "Yes. Of course. It's this: as I've said, you've got the *receptive* and the *constructive* functions of the brain. But when the brain receives sensory data, straight away it has to do *some* construction in order to *recognise* it as being sensory data. Are you still with me?"

"As much as we ever were," George assured him.

His brain clearly being unable to construct 'irony' from the sensory input, Trevor took this as a 'yes'. "Good," he said. "Now, the paradox I'm faced with arises because I need the biofeedback signal to help me attain a state of what I now call cerebral limbo, but the very reception of the signal rules out being in cerebral limbo. And this is where you fellows come in. I can't monitor the final stage through feedback, since that feedback will constitute my brain still performing a form of constructive activity – so I'm asking you two to act as monitors!"

"No problem," said George. "I used to be milk monitor at primary school."

"And I was blackboard monitor," I added.

Trevor looked at us suspiciously. "I do hope you fellows are taking this seriously," he snapped.

"We are," we assured him mendaciously.

"Good. Your task as monitors will be to switch off the biofeedback signal at the critical point so I can enter cerebral limbo. Got that?"

"Got it," I said.

"You must have had trial runs?" George said. "What happened with them?"

"Oh, some interesting phenomena," Trevor said vaguely. "Reminiscent of the accounts you find in the writings of the more esoteric Eastern mystics."

That sounded intriguing – did he develop strange new powers? The ability to levitate? See God? But he wouldn't explain further, dismissing us to our rooms and asking us to return to the lab in a couple of hours' time.

When George and I returned to the lab at the appointed hour, we were met by the revolting sight of Trevor clad in…well, clad in nothing but an obscene pair of lime-green Speedos and lime-green plastic footwear. He would easily have won a Gollum lookalike contest, with the real Gollum coming a distant second.

"Why the fancy dress?" I asked.

"Fancy *un*dress," said George.

"Flotation tank," Trevor said curtly. "Sensory deprivation. Reduce to a minimum all sensory input."

He would, we gathered, be buoyed up in the tank by the fluid it contained, which had a carefully calibrated density to match the average density of the subject, namely Trevor. As he floated there, any clothing would cause unwanted fluctuations in the signals sent to his brain by the touch receptors in his skin. These needed to be eliminated as far as possible. So he needed, in essence, to be naked in the tank, having discarded the Speedos, along with the footwear, once he had entered it. The temperature inside the floatation tank was automatically controlled, as was the air supply, which underwent filtering and renewing in a twenty-minute cycle. "You fellows don't have to concern yourself with that," he assured us. "There's a fail-safe back-up, which in turn has its own fail-safe back-up."

"And so on *ad infinitum*," George added.

I asked about the observation window – surely light entering the tank through the window would be a problem? But he had that covered; once settled in the tank, he would flick a switch and some electronic wizardry would render the window opaque. The only light inside the tank would be very low-level for the sake of the installed cameras, and to deal with that Trevor held up an eye mask. "One hundred per cent lightproof," he said.

The cameras in the tank would film everything, which we could view on a plasma screen occupying most of an end wall of the lab. Trevor wielded a remote control, and instantly the screen sprang to life. We could see the interior of the floatation tank at about twice life-size. The clarity was exceptional, except for one fuzzy patch which George pointed to.

"Er, it's pixellated," Trevor explained, sounding awkward.

"Why?"

"Well, I'll be lying in, or rather on, the fluid, and that is where…well, it's all being recorded as I say, so that will – well, protect my modesty." And for the first time ever I saw him redden.

"But with not much to be modest about," George muttered.

Trevor was opening a metal cupboard, from which he took out an item that proved to be basically a bathing cap but enhanced with numerous wires projecting from all over its surface. Each wire terminated in a USB connector. When Trevor donned it, he told us, it would be able to pick up brainwave activity from multiple locations inside his skull; and with the connectors secured to a bank of USB ports inside the floatation tank, all that information would be fed to recording equipment, as well as being displayed on the plasma screen.

Trevor pointed to the screen. Two oscilloscope patterns were displayed on either side of the main display.

"When I enter the tank," he told us, "I'll plug myself in, get in position on the fluid, then switch the observation window to non-transparency. That means I'll be entering full sensory deprivation mode. Now, the right-hand 'scope monitors my brain's *receptive* activity. The left-hand 'scope monitors my brain's *constructive* activity. The signal on the right-hand 'scope will drop rapidly, because my brain will be receiving little data from outside my body except the feedback signal. The left-hand 'scope signal will drop more slowly as biofeedback control nullifying my brain's constructive activity takes over. The time will come when the only constructive activity of my brain is its reception of the biofeedback signal. That's when the signal must be turned off, and I will enter cerebral limbo, able to choose and construct reality itself! Your task—"

"Should we choose to accept it," George murmured.

"—is to switch off the monitoring signal when the signal on the left-hand 'scope has flatlined for an hour."

He sounded triumphant. I felt puzzled, and George looked it.

"But surely all that could be done electronically," George then said, voicing an objection the two of us had discussed over the previous two hours. "That's what Paul and I don't get. Presiding genius of the Electronics Society relying on a couple of thickos like us, when you could easily whip up some fancy electronic circuitry to do it for you."

"Well, of course I could," Trevor said with some asperity. "Nothing easier! But" —and his tone softened— "I thought, well, I'd rather like you fellows to be around – witnesses and all that, as you were for my first forays into computers way back when." He looked rather sad for a moment, like a little boy wishing he had some friends to play with. "And you'd actually have a hand in the culmination of my life's work. I thought you'd like that."

"Of course, of course!" I said quickly.

"Where's this switch, then?" George asked.

It was located on top of a post, separate from all the other work surfaces, and required a key to be turned before it could be activated.

"And what happens then?" I asked.

"What happens is what happens! I will be constructing my own reality. Now, time for action."

He started rubbing some jelly stuff from a tube into the bald patches on his scalp, explaining it would ensure good electrical contact with the electrodes positioned inside the bathing cap, which he then put on. George held the tangle of wires for him. He mounted the little metal ladder, opened the hatch of the floatation tank, and entered. George handed up the wires.

"Just plugging them in," Trevor called out from within the tank. "And now let's get these off…"

A minute later, the repulsive lime-green Speedos and footwear were tossed out of the hatch. His top half appeared in the hatch opening, he gave a thumbs up, then he disappeared again, closing the hatch. Both through the observation window and on the plasma screen we could see him flick a series of switches. Something started humming. Complex wave patterns danced across the two oscilloscope images. We watched as he settled horizontally on the floatation tank fluid. His eyes were masked.

"All set." His voice came out of a couple of speakers.

George took up the microphone, by means of which we could speak to him. "This is lab control to Major Trev," he sang, sounding nothing like Bowie. "Time—"

"Be quiet, you fellows! I'm now switching the mic off and darkening the window."

A click, and the microphone went dead. The observation window went opaque, like highly reactive photochromic sunglasses. On the plasma screen we could see him lying on the floatation fluid like the carving of a mediaeval knight on his tomb. Mercifully, the pixellated area was accurately positioned…

George produced a bottle of malt from his jacket pocket, and I produced two glasses filched from the kitchen, into each of which he poured a generous measure. We clinked glasses.

"Here's to the past," I said.

"And to the future," said George.

The oscilloscope images continued to display a series of complex waveforms for twenty minutes or so, but we became aware that the complexity was slowly changing, simplifying. Trevor himself, as we could see on the screen, looked totally tranquil.

George and I spoke little. We had brought a chess set and started a game, but by unspoken consent we soon abandoned it. I wandered round the lab, peering at things, being generally nosy, while George started doing stuff on his mobile phone. We drank more whisky.

After about forty minutes the right-hand 'scope seemed to be flatlining. We turned up the sensitivity to find that it still showed a definite wave pattern, though now simply of an erratic sine wave. The left-hand 'scope still displayed a complex waveform.

More whisky.

An hour and a quarter after Trevor had entered the floatation tank, the right-hand 'scope was definitely flatlining, even when turned up to eleven. The left-hand 'scope now showed a much simpler waveform, and gradually the waveforms being traced out grew flatter and flatter. We turned up the sensitivity on that 'scope as well. The signal was almost flat, but not quite.

Another half hour passed. The bottle of whisky was half-empty. It was an excellent malt.

Then George, studying the oscilloscope images, said, "What do you reckon? No change for ages."

I looked. The monitoring signal was now barely registering, and I agreed that it had been unchanged for the stipulated time.

"Looks like we're there," muttered George. "It's weird, isn't it? D'you think he's reached his whatsit? Cerebral limbo?"

"When we switch off the monitoring signal," I said.

"Are you going to or shall I?"

"I'll turn the key, you press the switch. Then he'll have to include us both in his memoirs."

Which is what we did.

At first nothing happened. Then through the loudspeaker there came a faint sighing sound, as from another planet. Intensely melancholic. As the sigh faded away, I saw on the screen that Trevor's face and body had taken on a luminous quality, as though a light were beginning to shine beneath the skin. I looked at his hands which lay, one of them half on top of the other, on his stomach. They too seemed to be shining. I could see the cells of his skin, the structure of his skin, and below his skin I could see the blood vessels, the nerves, the muscles; then the bones became visible, as in an X-ray machine, then it seemed I could see inside the bones to their core, and it was like looking into the depths of space. His face too was becoming transparent, attenuated, as though its very substance was fading like an old photograph, but vastly quicker. I felt he was an unfathomable distance from us.

There was a rushing or whistling sound from the loudspeakers, like a sudden exhalation, then abruptly the observation window lit up with a violently bright white light – an intense, all-pervading radiance bleaching out, blotting out, every visible distinction in the lab. The entire lab became simply and overpoweringly a vessel of light, horribly painful to the eyes. I sank to my knees. I heard George gasping.

No sound, no heat. Just unadulterated light for what felt like an intolerable age. Then, just as abruptly, it vanished. No gentle fading away. Just *whap!* Gone!

For several minutes I lay on the floor, dazed. Then a noise. A voice. A croaky, trembling voice.

"Paul? Paul? You all right?"

I managed, slowly, to sit up. George was halfway to standing up – crouching like a sprinter waiting for the starting pistol. His eyes were screwed up.

I managed to say that yeah, I was okay, I think. "You?" I asked.

"Guess so. What the hell happened?"

"Don't know. Some power overload?"

There was a dim light in the laboratory – the emergency lights had come on. All the regular lights were extinguished, and the plasma screen was inert.

George stood, then staggered to the floatation tank and hauled himself up the metal ladder to the hatch. He hammered on it.

"Trev? Trevor? Trev? You all right, mate? What's going on?"

I managed to get to my feet. Apart from flickering after-images, I appeared to be unscathed. In my wandering around the lab earlier I had noticed some torches in their cradles – the rechargeable type that car mechanics use for working under a car – and, while George continued hammering on the hatch and calling to Trevor, I located two of them and joined George. He was now wrestling with the handle on the hatch which seemed to be either locked or jammed, but then it suddenly gave way and he nearly fell off the ladder. I steadied him.

Trembling, we shone the torches inside the tank, fearing we would find a dead or, at the very least, an unconscious Trevor.

The tank was empty. Well, empty of anything human. It was still half-full of the floatation fluid, and bobbing up and down on the fluid were the bathing cap and the eye mask. But of Trevor? Nothing. Trevor, I repeat, was not there, dead or alive or anything in-between. He was not on the surface of the liquid, he was not drifting about in the bulk of the liquid, he had not sunk to the bottom.

Trevor had vanished.

The obvious thing to do, we realised after we had finished George's whisky double quick, retired to the kitchen, made some ghastly substitute for coffee and shakingly drunk it, all the while repeating that none of this made sense – the obvious thing to do would be to replay the recording that had been made of the evening's events; that would surely show us what had happened in the floatation tank, what had happened to Trevor. But when we came to play back the recording, we discovered that the machine was a total wreck. It had been transformed into a mass of fused metal – the result, presumably, of receiving a concentrated blast of intense power. Absolutely nothing usable remained, which meant that George and I alone would be able to give any sort of account of the previous few hours in the laboratory of Trevor Baring.

Later, we worked out what must have happened. To do so we used Trevor's own line of reasoning, and discovered the flaw in his argument. He had maintained that what we know as reality is only the result of the constructive activity of the brain. But if that is so, then abolishing all constructive activity automatically involved abolishing all reality for the participant. The 'cerebral limbo' for which Trevor aimed – and which he presumably entered upon our switching off the monitoring signal – was not, as he supposed, a state from which he could choose to construct his own reality; it was in fact a state of no reality at all. In willing his brain to be free from *all* sensory data, he had willed the abolition of his reality. There being no reality for him in which to exist, he himself could no longer exist.

He did not die, he simply ceased to be.

Trevor had thought himself out of existence.

That is the only explanation George and I could come up with which accounts for all the facts, and will of course be the central plank in our defence against the charges (even in the absence of a body) of conspiracy to murder and actual murder.

Our case comes up next week. Our legal team holds out little hope, particularly because the prosecution has apparently got hold of Beth, who is going to testify that George and I have held a grudge against Trevor for decades, ever since the days of the Electronics Society. Nonsense, of course, but regrettably she has kept an indiscreet email I sent her after tracking her down on Friends Reunited, containing – among other things – my libellous opinion of Trevor. A facetious missive, needless to say, but it doesn't read well.

Our best chance, apparently, is if our case is tried by Judge Schrödinger. With him we'll have a fifty-fifty chance of being acquitted. Although I don't like to think about the alternative, *not thinking* could be a mistake: if what happened to Trevor is anything to go by, *not* to think gets you, quite literally, nowhere.

The Lure of the Footlights

Prologue

The opening number, *Hand Me My Cap and Bells*, was, without being wildly hilarious, definitely promising, with the seven performers exuding energy and confidence and sheer *joie de vivre*. As they departed into the wings at its conclusion, Phil Ellis, along with the rest of the audience in the packed hall, clapped vigorously. The applause had not fully died down when two of the performers reappeared, pushing an enormous pram, and launched into a comic song about a baby having an "unmarried, undergraddy daddy for a mummy" and a "bachelor undergrad for a dad". A clever, witty lyric with a catchy tune practically demanding audience participation, and a wildly funny pay-off when a frilly-bonneted apparition in baby clothes suddenly sat bolt upright in the pram, raucously squawking the final chorus and manically waving an oversized baby's rattle at the audience as he was being wheeled off. Phil, occupying a seat next to the central aisle, almost fell off it laughing. Instantly – or so it seemed, although this was probably an illusion fostered by the continuing applause and cheering which gave the performers extra time – the former occupant of the pram returned to the front of the stage, now wearing a stylish dark blue jacket with gold braid on it, his baby's bonnet discarded in favour of a peaked cap. He had mutated into a pilot with the airline *Alitalia* – the title of the sketch – giving instructions to his passengers in broken English. With his highly mobile, expressive features he elicited laughs not only with the lines he was uttering but also with every twitch of an eyebrow, every sidelong glance, every despairing curl of the lip. Phil could barely breathe for laughing so much. The man in the seat next to him was baying with laughter; those in front of him and those across the aisle were likewise howling; the entire hall had become an alchemist's alembic, transmuting the lead of a typescript into comedy gold.

Here he was. Early September 1969. At the Edinburgh Festival fringe. In a hall holding maybe two hundred people. Watching a late-night show: the Cambridge University Footlights revue. 'An Hour Late', directed by Clive James. Phil had not heard of him before, but according to the programme notes James had recently been president of the Footlights.

A few days previously, Phil had hitch-hiked to Edinburgh specifically to see the show in anticipation of starting at Cambridge University that October, where he would be reading for a Natural Sciences degree. But his main ambition was to join the Footlights club, the training ground over the years of so many high-profile comedians. Having heard on the radio and watched on TV many of the comedy greats who had emanated from the club, he had wanted to see the current crop in the flesh; to be in the presence of their aura, their glory; to pay homage to them; to genuflect before them; to imagine himself on stage with them; to feel himself, at least potentially, *one of them*.

The Italian pilot sketch was succeeded by a musical parody, followed by a one-off gag about a policeman, then a double act with Field Marshal Montgomery and Earl Mountbatten – 'Monty and Mounty'. All so quick and snappy, so slick, so beautifully crafted, so weepingly funny. As he laughed, Phil became dimly aware that he was being swept up into something transcendently greater than himself; the entire audience had become one single vast organism melded from two hundred or more disparate entities. The fact that he, Phil, had come on his own, that he did not know the name of anyone else in the audience, meant nothing, for they laughed as one, applauded as one, cheered as one.

Intoxicating stuff.

The pace never slackened: verbal comedy, physical comedy, extended sketches, one-gag quickies, with the occasional musical item to give the enthralled audience brief recovery periods before plunging it back into the maelstrom of laughter. No interval, which surely would have dissipated the energy. No let-up in the waves of joyous emotion like an almighty sea beating on the cliffs…but then, far too soon, for it should not be allowed ever to end, came the show's final sketch: a wrestling match depicted in a slow-motion replay, which took the entire show to an unsurpassable climax.

After a closing number, the cast took several curtainless curtain calls. The atmosphere was terrific, with clapping, cheering, whistling, the stamping of feet. Phil clapped and cheered and whistled and foot-stamped along with everyone else, feeling as he did so that he had become profoundly and permanently connected with every single person present, cast members and the audience alike, in one huge love-in.

The performers gave a final wave and jauntily withdrew to the wings, but the acclamation continued until, with no sign of their returning, it slowly subsided, coats and bags were gathered, and a general move toward the exits began. Phil, longingly, reluctantly, was one of the last to leave.

The cold night air – it had gone midnight, though he had lost all sense of time – did not trouble him as he headed for his lodgings on the outskirts of the city. The walk was welcome, as lines and sketches from the revue spontaneously replayed themselves before his inner eye and inner ear. He repeatedly laughed afresh.

Arriving at the house where he had a small room for the four nights of his Edinburgh stay – and this was his final night – he quickly made himself a tea in the kitchen, then headed up the stairs. He sat on the bed, drinking the tea and slowly calming down. The revue was no longer spontaneously replaying itself in his head, though he knew he could easily call to mind specific parts of it if he chose. Yet as he calmed down he became increasingly aware that, alongside the intense joy of it all, another, less welcome, feeling had made an appearance, like the spreading of a stain. A despondency, a dejection. Verbally, though it did not present itself to him in words so much as in a state of painful perception, it amounted to: *how on earth could he ever hope to match, or even come remotely close to, the standard of material he had seen performed? It was way beyond his abilities. How could he have the presumption to believe he could write and perform stuff at their level?* The sketches he had been trying to write over the past few months to impress the Footlights when he started at Cambridge in a few weeks' time – well, they were so much junk, weren't they? If what he had just seen was the level of brilliance required, then it was hopeless.

He got into bed and curled up. The dejection coexisted with the joy; it did not banish it. He could still recall instantly the look on the Alitalia pilot's face when he lugubriously explained that "the wings – they shrink!" Or Montgomery claiming that "the men loved me, by George! And each other by rota!" Or the hysterical lunacy of the slow-motion wrestling… Yes, joy continued to well up at their memory…yet still a dejection permeated the joy.

*

In later years, Phil Ellis could not precisely date when the desire to be a member of the Cambridge Footlights had first taken hold. He retained a vague memory of making his mother laugh by strumming an imaginary guitar along to a record playing on the radio. He must have been five or six at the time. He had no recollection of what the record was but guessed it would have been an early rock and roll number by someone like Bill Haley, whom he had seen on *Pathé News* at the cinema. Encouraged by his mother, he had repeated the performance more than once, making his father, his aunt and uncle and, most important of all, his cousin Sam laugh as well. Her approval led him to look for other ways of making her and other people laugh. He liked words and was quick with them, and when he had to wait at the barber's for his turn, he would sit reading the jokes in the tatty magazines supplied, memorising not only those that made him laugh but also those which sounded clever, even if he didn't quite understand them. Making Sam and school friends laugh at them, or giggle, or even be puzzled by them until he had explained what was funny or clever brought him little bursts of happiness he wanted to be repeated.

When the radio comedy programme *I'm Sorry, I'll Read That Again* was broadcast in the 1960s he followed it avidly, and on the day after an episode he and his fellow addicts at school would endlessly rehearse the jokes and sketches, often to the incomprehension and irritation of classmates who were not fans of the show. Those in on it would try to emulate the radio performers with their own appalling jokes and wordplays. Phil was proud of his growing reputation as creator of many of the best – that is to say, worst – puns.

At some stage he discovered, though how or from whom he also never subsequently remembered, that *I'm Sorry* had its origins in a revue mounted at Cambridge University by members of a club called Footlights. An institution of which, he also learned, his hero Peter Cook, from the television show *Not Only... But Also*, had once been the president. Footlights alumni appeared on other shows he watched: *The Frost Report, At Last the 1948 Show, Twice a Fortnight, Do Not Adjust Your Set...* Extracts from a Footlights revue featuring current members, broadcast on television in a half-hour programme, made him fall about with laughter and envy.

A vague wish that he could join the Footlights suddenly became a realistic ambition when he learned that the school staff thought that, although he had spent his school career up to O levels in the B form – thanks to his indifferent performance in subjects like history, geography, French, Latin and woodwork – he had a good chance of winning a place at Cambridge University to read science. Following their advice he applied to Pembroke College, and in due course was called for an interview, along with Rob Wilson, another from the science sixth. Phil knew him as a genial, scholarly character who played the guitar and whose ambition, he had discovered, lay in the direction of getting into the music scene. Phil was keeping to himself his hopes of the Footlights.

In early September they travelled by train across country, discussing what questions they might get asked and how to avoid starting every answer with 'Well', then walked along the Backs beside the river to kill time before their interviews. At last, Phil endured an anxiety-ridden hour or more being cross-questioned about his extra-curricular activities and academic ambitions, about which he said "Well…" several times. On their return journey to Devon he gloomily prognosticated to Rob that he'd be sent the academic equivalent of a 'Dear John' letter. Rob, cautiously optimistic about his own chances, reminded him that there were still the scholarship exams to sit, the results of which could lead to the offer of a place. Not everything depended on the interview alone.

These exams came in late November, and he emerged from them feeling no more optimistic than before. His gloom continued. A few days before Christmas the letter arrived from the college, beginning, "Dear Mr Ellis, I regret to inform you," – and he groaned. He'd totally buggered it up. Oh well – "that we are unable to offer you a scholarship to the College," he forced himself to read, "but we are pleased to offer you an ordinary place. Should you choose to accept this offer…"

"Fucking Ada!" he yelled in a burst of gloom-banishing amazement, forgetting that he believed his parents didn't know he swore.

Twenty minutes later, Rob rang. He too would be going to Cambridge.

ii

Phil had left school at the end of that term. Impelled by the need for extra book and beer money to supplement the local authority grant he'd be getting, he successfully applied for a temporary post as a lab assistant with a biochemical research company. He started in the new year. At the same time, Rob began work with a company specialising in electronic equipment.

Since the previous September, their relationship had developed from that of being friendly fellow pupils to that of a good friendship. They now saw each other regularly, and Phil had let slip to him about his Footlights ambition. One evening when Rob had invited him round, he found another school acquaintance present. He knew Greg Adams only slightly, since Greg, like Rob, had until the sixth form been in the A stream. Tall and amiable, Greg, known at school for being an exceptionally talented artist, had already begun accepting commissions.

Over coffee, Rob revealed that Greg had some information about the Footlights for Phil. "Apparently," he said, "you can't just turn up, slip them five guineas or twenty doubloons or however much they sting you for, and in you go. You have to go through some sort of initiation ceremony first. Isn't that it?" he appealed to Greg.

Greg nodded. He was slouched in a chair, legs stretched out. "A cousin of mine was a member a few years back. I checked with him when Rob mentioned you're hoping to join." He paused.

"And?" said Phil impatiently.

"Ah yes, sorry. What you have to do, he said, is you have to write some material – a sketch or so – and perform it in front of them, and if they like it they invite you to join the club."

"And if they don't?"

Greg drew a finger across his throat. "You're cast into the outer darkness, where there's a wailing and gnashing of teeth."

Phil laughed. "But seriously," he said. "When you say 'perform in front of them', who's 'them'?"

"Ah well, what happens is they have evening concerts, called 'smokers', two or three times a term, and you have to audition to appear in one of them, and that's just in front of two or three of the bigwigs. If you pass *that* audition, then you get to perform in front of the whole club, and that's when they decide whether to invite you to join. Or not," he added after another pause.

"Scary," said Phil as an image came to mind of standing alone in front of a stony-faced audience all holding up scorecards like judges on a TV show. What if you were faced with a forest of zeros? God, that would be so humiliating. What did you have to score to be invited to join the club? Were there grades, like A levels? Could he subject himself to such a terror?

"Cheers, Greg," he said. "That's helpful. Bit of a challenge, though."

"You can do it," Rob said encouragingly. "You're a punmeister. All you've got to do is put all your best ones together."

"That's what you're known for," said Greg. "If you want a good pun, apply to Ellis!"

"It's one thing making puns, though," Phil said, "and totally another to write an actual script and perform it."

"But it's what you want to do!" said Rob.

"Yep. So come on, let's come up with some ideas."

"I've an idea for a sketch or two," Greg offered languidly. He held up a sketching block.

"Nice one," Phil acknowledged.

As Phil and Rob talked comedy, Greg set about drawing the two friends from different angles. Rob suggested a sketch parodying their former headmaster addressing the school at the start of a new academic year; Phil himself wondered about Sir Isaac Newton addressing the Royal Society on his 'discovery of levity'. They tossed around other possibilities as Greg continued to draw.

More coffee. Greg showed them his drawings: clever caricatures of each of them. "My contribution," he said, tearing out the pages and handing them over.

The evening moved on to all three reminiscing about their former school, then concluded with Rob picking up his guitar and playing a song he'd recently written, lamenting the break-up with a girlfriend which had occurred several months previously. He rhymed her name, Anne, with 'also-ran' and 'brain scan'.

Over the next few evenings Phil sweated over the headmaster idea, knowing it to be an unoriginal concept plagiarised from a John Cleese sketch. The resulting farrago contained a series of feeble puns which he hoped would work by leading up to a couple of really big laughs, but an internal critical voice naggingly maintained that *they won't though, will they?* And despite being pleased with the reference to an invisible pupil called Crick who had *used the school labs to create a new type of furniture-protecting fluid, and varnished* – with the pay-off line, *Crick! You're a pain in the neck!* – he couldn't tell if even that would raise a laugh. The same critical voice assured him: *it won't.*

However, he took the completed script round to Rob's for a second and, with Greg also being there, a third opinion. Rob chuckled politely three or four times, saying at its completion, "I really like the line about Crick. A good scientific name. You can't get Watson in there somewhere as well?" He was biting the skin at the side of his fingernails.

"I thought it was funny," Greg said, looking up from his ever-present sketch pad. "But what do I know?"

"You didn't exactly *laugh*," Phil said.

"I was laughing inside," said Greg. "I can't laugh out loud and draw at the same time."

Phil sighed. "It's crap, isn't it?"

"I wouldn't say that!" said Rob.

"Only because you're a clean-living bugger who doesn't use that sort of language."

"Not at all. It just needs a bit more work."

"It needs some decent bloody jokes."

"Them too."

"Must have a bash at Newton," Phil decided, and Rob played him a Leonard Cohen number. Greg had returned to his sketch pad.

The following week Phil laboured every evening over the Newton sketch.

"Crap rating?" he asked Rob after reading it to him. Greg was not present on this occasion.

"Definite improvement," said Rob.

But still not much good, said the critical voice, as Rob played another recently composed song, this time about the joys of having a new girlfriend. He rhymed her name, Natalie, with *chattily* and *fantastically*.

iii

The weeks passed. The lab work went well: with no exams looming, he enjoyed the relaxed atmosphere, the lack of competitiveness, the routine and the pay. His beer and book fund grew, though not quite as fast as he had hoped.

His social life ticked over. Many of his school friends were not around, most of them having already gone off to their universities, returning briefly over the Easter break then disappearing again, and Rob was increasingly spending time with girlfriend Natalie. But there were a couple of others still around who, like him, were between school and Oxbridge, and hadn't headed off to exotic places for the duration but were in temporary jobs. They met at various pubs, at rock concerts in Exeter, at parties.

And there was cousin Sam. She lived in Teignford, a village not far from his own village of Silveridge, and the two of them had always been close. Cousins twice over, for their mothers were sisters and their fathers brothers, they had been born within a few weeks as well as a few miles of each other. They had almost been brought up together, what with frequent family get-togethers at weekends and birthdays and bank holidays, joint family holidays, and – from their early teens onwards – one or other of them often cycling over to the other's house or heading out onto Dartmoor together. For the first twelve years of her life Sam had been, like Phil, an only child; then her mother had given birth to twin boys, who for several subsequent years had been a cause of concern with a string of health problems. During that period, Sam had spent even more time with Phil's family to take pressure off her parents.

A sparky girl, practically minded and with no desire for prolonging her academic education, she had, after A levels, started work in the repair centre run by her father, Phil's uncle Jack. She could be very feminine when she chose, though always with a dash of the tomboy, and Phil suspected she was happiest when, in overalls and with her long, darkish hair gathered up into a hairnet, she was immersed in the intricacies of farm machinery. He fancied her in an ill-defined way.

On his birthday at the end of June – his last as a teenager – he took her out for a meal, along with Rob and Natalie. Afterwards, when Rob asked if he and Sam were serious, he told him how they were double cousins, and said, "Do the genetics."

"Normal for Devon?" Rob suggested.

At a family gathering in mid-August to celebrate Sam's own nineteenth birthday, her father toasted her, saying what an asset she was to his business and announcing proudly, "I've never seen anyone learn faster how to strip a JCB."

"Lucky old JCB!" Phil whispered to his cousin as everyone else present drank the toast.

Sam spluttered. "Naughty boy!" she whispered back.

"What are you two sniggering about?" her father enquired.

"The universe and all that surrounds it," Phil said in the voice of Peter Cook's alter ego, E. L. Wisty.

At the end of the evening, with the rest of the family still gossiping over coffee in the cottage, Phil and Sam wandered off into the large garden with its fruit cages and vegetable beds and outhouses, talking of what might be lying in store for each of them during the rest of the year. Sam already knew of his Footlights ambition and how he intended to go to the Edinburgh Festival fringe to see their revue, as a prelude to joining, or attempting to join, the club itself.

"Have you decided exactly when you're going?" she asked.

"Three weeks today."

"And you're definitely hitching?"

"No reason not to." He mimed hitching a lift.

"Well, you take care!"

"You sure you can't come?" He had already asked her several times if she would be able to go with him. "Show a bit of roadside leg?" He expanded his mime to suggest the twitching of a skirt.

"Hey!" Sam gave him a push. "Is that all you want me for? My legs?"

"There's no answer to that. But you're sure you can't come?"

"I'm so sorry, coz." Sam sounded genuinely regretful. "It'd be fun, but I really can't. Dad's going to need me here – he's short-handed as it is." She put her arms round him and kissed him on the cheek. "You'll be fine on your own – and I won't be there to cramp your style. You'll meet some gorgeous chick at some show – just you see."

"I wish."

iv

There were about twenty others present, nineteen or twenty years old, and all – like Phil himself – casually dressed, mainly in jeans or cords. Only two young women were present, dressed in a slightly hippy fashion: long flowing skirts and patchwork tunics. Two out of twenty – that pretty much reflected the ratio throughout the university in general. The atmosphere was nervy, like waiting to be let into the exam hall for A levels, with no one knowing what to say, if anything, to anyone else, except for the two young women who had arrived together and were chatting in low voices.

They were gathered in the clubroom of the Cambridge Footlights. Smaller than Phil had been expecting, it was on the first floor of a building in Falcon Yard, a rather dingy location in the centre of the city. The ground floor of the building – as a faint but definite odour of the piscine announced – acted as a warehouse for a wholesale fishmonger, and the clubroom itself was accessed by a somewhat creepy little staircase. Occasional thudding sounds were coming through the ceiling from whatever took place on the top floor.

The far end of the clubroom featured a stage half-hidden by a single unprepossessing curtain, its drooping partner drawn back to the wings. Posters of Footlights revues over the years decorated the walls: *A Clump of*

Plinths, Supernatural Gas, Stuff What Dreams Are Made Of, Turns of the Century and others. Stacks of chairs had been pushed untidily against the walls, and a small bar occupied the near end of the room, where the two hosts for the meeting were pouring drinks. One was tall, curly-haired and loose-limbed, the other short and compact, with spectacles. Phil recognised them as having been in the Edinburgh revue.

Arriving in the first week of October, Phil had been in Cambridge less than two weeks. The days since then had been full on: settling into his room in Pembroke New Court; attending a drinks reception with the Master; enjoying a 'Formal Hall' for all freshers; meeting his Director of Studies; tramping round the city with Rob, who insisted on using a map, which betrayed their fresher status; renting a typewriter; visiting school friends at Trinity and Downing Colleges; joining the Cambridge Union; and watching in awe the first episode of *Monty Python's Flying Circus* in a packed Junior Common Room.

He had drunk strong coffee numerous times with fellow freshers, and over-indulged in the JCR bar on a couple of occasions. And, with Rob, he had gone along to the Societies' Fair, where a seemingly infinite number of university-approved clubs, societies, unions, groups, parties, associations and the like advertised themselves, seeking to sign up new members. While Rob had wandered around looking for musical organisations, Phil had only one thing in mind: Footlights. Finding the stall displaying the motto *Ars Est Celare Artem*, which his O level Latin just about allowed him to translate as 'the art is to conceal the art', he waited until a group of six or seven other freshers had dispersed, then approached the amiable-looking guardian of the mysteries. He had no pamphlets, leaflets, application forms or any informative literature whatsoever, but responded cheerfully enough to Phil's enquiry with the suggestion that he attend a meeting at the clubroom the following week. And he did at least tell him where to find the clubroom.

Phil had been the first to arrive for the meeting. He had spent a few minutes flicking through a large hardback notebook labelled *Comments & Suggestions* that was lying on a table near the entrance. On one page a club member had suggested as the title for a May Week revue *Biggles Flies Apart!* Someone else had altered it to *Biggles' Flies Undone!* Earlier in the book, he had found and smiled at a reminder, entered a couple of years previously, that Prince Charles had joined the club and that no sketches should be performed making fun of him, since, as a member of the royal family, "he already has enough disadvantages to put up with."

As the bespectacled host handed out the drinks, the tall one called those who were wandering round the room to come and take a seat, then he himself sat in a decayed-looking armchair and addressed the ragged circle of young hopefuls in front of him.

"Welcome, everyone! It's very good to see you all. I'm Adrian, the president, and the drinks wallah is Bill, who doubles up on his day off as the vice president."

"No jokes about 'vice', please," Bill put in. "I've heard them all."

Phil did not join in the murmur of obsequious laughter, which was in any case abruptly drowned out by a burst of thudding coming through the ceiling, accompanied by a brief twanging of (presumably) an electric guitar.

"Okay," the president continued. "You're all here because you've expressed an interest in the Footlights, and may be hoping to become members." Nods all round, including from Phil. "Bill and I are going to fill you in on the procedure, because as you probably know it's not like other Cambridge societies – you can't just sign up, pay the subscription and become a member simply because you want to. We're going to put you in the picture of how—"

Another outbreak of thudding and twanging caused him to pause for a few seconds, saying when the racket ceased, "I'll continue provided I'm allowed to by…" To finish the sentence, he simply pointed up at the ceiling.

"By God?" Phil said quickly.

People laughed. The president of the Footlights laughed. The vice president of the Footlights laughed. Fellow aspirants to membership of the Footlights laughed. Not that loudly and not that long, because obviously it wasn't hugely funny; but he had been quick, had got the tone of voice and delivery just right – and the resultant laughter had sounded genuine. Phil caught the eye of the sexier of the two young women, whose jet-black hair was cut pageboy style. She was smiling slightly. He resolutely kept his face straight and did not look round at the rest of the group.

"A disco," the president explained. "And a rehearsal room some group uses. More amenable than God."

"Moving in a mysterious way," another of the aspirants offered, but his line, to Phil's relief, failed to raise a second laugh.

"They're checking their equipment," Bill said. "I'll go and have a word."

As he left the room, Adrian resumed his explanation of how to achieve membership of the club. Phil realised that his early nervousness had vanished. He had actually made the president of the Cambridge Footlights laugh. Did this mean that his main ambition in applying to Cambridge University would be realised? To follow in the Footlit footsteps of Peter Cook, John Cleese, Tim Brooke-Taylor; to write and perform comedy and make people laugh as helplessly as he had laughed at the Edinburgh revue only a few weeks ago?

The president's explanation confirmed what Greg had told him at Rob's months ago: write a sketch, perform it in front of the club members at an evening smoker, and wait to be invited if the committee members thought you good enough. Would he be good enough? Well, he had written three possible sketches already – would at least one of them pass muster? Raise enough laughs to prove his worth? The dejection he had experienced along with the joy at the revue in Edinburgh had lifted somewhat – though not very confident, he had regularly reminded himself that he was *a bloody B former who had overcome the odds and made it to Cambridge* – and he could damn well overcome the odds again.

And he had already made the president of the Footlights laugh. Not a bad start.

v

Two days later, after a morning of lectures, Phil returned to college and headed for the JCR. As on most days, various invitations had accumulated in his pigeonhole – the Pembroke Christian Union, the Pembroke Debating Society, Bridge Club, Choir, Film Society and others. After a cursory inspection, they joined the litter of identical invitations already encircling the wastepaper bin like the outcome of a card-flicking game played by incompetents. He retained a leaflet about the Pembroke Players, the college theatrical group, and an invitation to tea with the Dean, his designated 'moral tutor', whatever that alarming designation entailed. Such an 'invitation' was more in the nature of a royal summons.

Far more important, though, was a real letter addressed to him in Sam's handwriting. A surprise – she had never been much of a letter writer. Was she missing him? On his return from Edinburgh they'd spent a number of evenings together, and a couple of Dartmoor rambles, before he'd come up to Cambridge – not romantic, they didn't do romance – but this was the first time he'd been in a situation when he wouldn't see and couldn't see her for weeks on end, and it felt odd. As though something unspecified had been extracted from him, but under an anaesthetic which hadn't quite worn off because it wasn't actually painful, just…just odd. Puzzling. Perhaps she felt the same. And maybe she could come and visit, despite the archaic college rule about no female visitors after midnight, and *certainly* not staying overnight. Maybe that was the function of moral tutors – to police the sex lives of undergraduates and maintain the purity of college members. As it were.

He took the letter into the television room – already occupied by a scattering of said members – opened the poorly sealed envelope and drew out Sam's letter. It consisted of a single sheet of writing paper headed *Ellis & Co: Farm Machinery Repairs*, accompanied by a newspaper cutting.

Hi coz!

How are you? Working hard? All's well here but busy – I spent yesterday stripping (a JCB!!). Missing you! [There followed a few snippets of family news, then:] *I saw the enclosed in some rag and thought of you. You might already have come across it, but I wondered if it's something you could use for a sketch.*

Have you got an audition for the Footlights yet? When? I'll be thinking of you!

Lots of love
Sam xxxxx
P.S. met any gorgeous chicks yet??

He unfolded the newspaper cutting, which bore the headline 'Welsh team banned from the Soviet Union'. A filler item, it referred to a rugby team from a Welsh village which, having won a minor league, had, somewhat strangely, received an invitation to go on a short tour in the Soviet Union and play half a dozen games. The tour never took place: they had been barred from entering when the Soviet officials, not believing that so many people – over half the squad – could all be called Jones, had suspected some Western imperialist plot and revoked their visas.

Phil laughed out loud. "Jones passes to Jones," he said quietly but with rising emphasis, "who passes to Jones, who passes to Jones!"

"Sorry?" someone said in a loud Welsh accent. Phil looked up to find another of the JCR occupants frowning at him. Roger Evans, Phil recalled – a rugby-playing hearty, well known in the college for his foghorn voice and emphasising his Welshness.

"Nothing to worry about," Phil said, getting up.

"I wasn't worrying, boyo! Just hope you're not going mental!"

Inspiration trumping hunger, he gave lunch a miss and jogged his way to his rooms. As he passed by the area known as the Dean's Garden, packed with exotic vegetation and a hidden pond with a reputation of luring drunken undergraduates to a watery fine, he repeated out loud, "Jones passes to Jones, who passes to Jones, who passes to Jones," then, with foghorn Roger coming to mind, he modified it to "Evans passes to Evans, who passes to Evans, who passes to Evans…" That sounded better. He couldn't have said why, but it did. Skirting the croquet lawn, he continued, "Evans passes to Evans, who crosses to Evans, who kicks to Evans…" *Much* better. Make it football, not rugby. Then, "Evans beats Evans, beats Evans, beats Evans, beats Evans…" Players of *both* teams had to be called Evans. All of them… "But here comes Evans, and Evans is tackling Evans, and Evans is down! Evans is on the ground, he's writhing on the ground…" Panting now as he closed in on the archway entrance to his staircase, he continued to ad lib. "And here comes the referee…he's taking someone's name… It's Evans!" he cried as he started up the stairs. "He's taking Evans' name! This is a disgrace – this lad Evans, always in trouble…"

By the time he reached his room, he was in a state of high excitement.

vi

At the end of the meeting in the clubroom, the Footlights aspirants had each been offered a time to return for an initial audition to show what material they had to offer, and possibly to be given advice on polishing it before a performance in front of the full club membership at the next smoker.

Phil's time slot was late on Monday afternoon. Following an hour with his maths supervisor, during which he felt he had acquitted himself more creditably than expected, he hurtled round to Falcon Yard, locked his bike to a drainpipe, hauled the pannier off the rack and charged his way up the creepy staircase, which still smelled of fish, to the clubroom. With him he had brought such scripts as he thought might stand a chance: the headmaster's speech, Isaac Newton's scientific paper on his theory of levity, and a television cook's surreal recipes. He also had the current version of the Evans sketch, but his initial enthusiasm for it had died away in reaction to a lukewarm opinion from Rob. He had subsequently added several bad puns to it, but would that be enough? Doubtful. He probably wouldn't offer Evans at the audition after all.

"Phil, come in!" Adrian the president beckoned him to where he and Bill, the vice president, were sitting in the middle of the room at a table covered in papers, some of which had spilled over onto the floor. "What have you got for us?"

"Three of them," Phil said, fumbling to draw a file out of the pannier, and hoping he wasn't coming across as nervous as he felt.

"That sounds promising," Bill said. He wore glasses halfway down his nose and was looking over the top of them. "Why don't you show us what you think is your best? No, no." He raised a prohibitive hand as Phil held out his headmaster script to him. "I do mean *show* us. Up on the stage. Perform it for us. Don't worry, it doesn't have to be done from memory or be particularly polished, but it'll give us some idea of its potential."

"Yeah, sure." Feeling annoyed with himself – *of course* they'd want to see him perform; that's what an audition entails, *idiot* – Phil made his way up the steps and onto the stage.

Script in one hand, he hooked the thumb of his other hand into the corresponding armpit, stepped forward and began. "Welcome back, school, to a new academic year, and may I say…"

The sketch moved on. Adrian chuckled at one point, Bill at another point. At no time did they chuckle in unison, let alone laugh loudly. Bill was making notes.

"All right," said Adrian at the end. "That's it? Well done. Come down and join us."

Fighting a strong urge to run to the door, scuttle down the stairs and never be seen again in Falcon Yard, Phil joined them at the table and, at Bill's request, handed him the script.

"Mmm," Bill said, glancing at it. "There were one or two nice lines in that."

"One or two," agreed Adrian, nodding, with what sounded to Phil like an unexpressed continuation, *but no more than one or two, if that.*

"But it hasn't got a real *oomph* anywhere that takes the audience by surprise," Bill explained. "Something you build up to. What else have you got in that file?"

Phil handed over Newton and the TV Cook, and watched anxiously as Adrian and Bill each read one in almost complete silence. His mouth had gone completely dry.

"Not bad," Adrian eventually said about Newton, "not bad. You really go in for tortuous puns, don't you?"

"I do rather," said Phil cautiously. Was this a good or bad thing?

"What do you reckon, Bill?" Adrian asked.

"I agree," Bill said in a tone that made it clear that it was not a good thing. "Have you got anything else? What's that?"

"It's one I'm still working on," said Phil, wishing he could just get the hell out of there. This was awful.

"Let's see it, then."

Phil reluctantly handed over the partially completed Evans sketch.

Bill started to read. A few seconds later he gave a brief bark of laughter. Another few seconds, and a delighted laugh. Bill glanced up at Phil, smiled, and resumed reading. He banged the table and laughed again, then laughed for several seconds without stopping, and nodded at Adrian. There came a stretch when he wasn't laughing but grinning and nodding, and Phil could see him mouthing the words, then a series of chuckles, culminating in a huge laugh at 'It's Evans! He's taking Evans' name!' A few more laughs followed before he handed the script to Adrian, who had been looking increasingly puzzled and impatient. Adrian started to read, and an identical sequence of reactions followed.

"All *right*!" said Adrian, placing the script on the table and tapping it decisively. "This is vastly better. This is quality. Bill?"

"Agreed." Bill took off his spectacles and briefly polished them. "You've got something here, Phil, you really have."

"I wasn't sure—" Phil started to say.

"Never easy to tell about your own stuff," Adrian interrupted. "Let's focus on this, then. All right?"

"All right," said Phil faintly.

For five or ten minutes Adrian and Bill studied and discussed the script. *Keep this to start with – this would be better later – how about moving this to here – what do you think, Phil? – lead up a little more slowly to this line here – cut that, another of his puns – breaks the flow – that's where the oomph is – yes, agreed...*

"What do you reckon, Phil?" Adrian eventually said. "Would you think of restructuring it along those lines? Up to you, of course."

"That's fantastic," Phil said, barely able to say anything coherent, overwhelmed as he was by their response. "But I don't know how to end it."

"It'd be good to have a strong laugh to end on," said Bill thoughtfully.

"I don't know so much," Adrian said. "This line here is so strong, I think he could just say, 'and with that, I hand you back to the studio'."

"And Dai Evans," Phil added spontaneously.

"Yes!" Bill shouted. "Lovely!"

It was agreed that Phil would take the script away and make a number of amendments along the lines they had been suggesting, and they would include him in the programme for the next smoker. "We'll put you near the beginning," Bill said, "so you're not waiting in agony the whole evening."

During the last few minutes of their discussion, Phil had noticed that the hippyish young woman with the pageboy haircut had arrived and was hovering near the door.

"Okay," Adrian said. "We need to leave it there. Thanks for coming in, Phil, and we'll see you at the smoker Friday week. Rebecca! Hi!" He beckoned to her. "Come on in."

As she approached the table, Phil realised she was breathing rapidly. He tried to say something reassuring to her, but was still too much in a daze to think of anything coherent.

He continued in a daze as he cycled back to college. He sat in his room in a daze. He kept replaying the audition in a daze. Eventually, emerging from his daze when it was too late to go into hall, he went to the communal kitchen and cooked himself beans on toast. On returning to his room, he sat down at the desk, put a fresh sheet of paper in the typewriter, and began to type a new draft of Evans.

vii

The clubroom bar was already doing good business when Phil arrived on the evening of the smoker, with loud, confident, mainly male voices putting in orders, and their owners waving ten shilling and pound notes at the bar steward. Alcohol, he knew, would be a bad idea at this stage, but even had he wanted a drink it would take too much effort to get one.

The atmosphere was noisy with talk, laughter, shouts and the sound of a honky-tonk piano; eponymous smoke from cigarettes, along with the odd cigar and even odder pipe, helped counteract any smell of fish wafting up from the ground floor. Seats in irregular rows filled the body of the room, many of them already occupied, while up on the stage the curtains twitched and flapped as harassed-looking individuals could be seen ineffectually pulling on cords and tugging the curtains directly. Phil, holding his bike pannier, looked around for someone – anyone – he might know, or at least recognise, to make contact with. The president and vice president were talking together near the stage, but he could hardly go up and hobnob with them, could he? Here and there were faces vaguely familiar from the preliminary meeting in this very room, and he had just decided to introduce himself to the nearest when a young woman's voice behind him asked him to let her get by.

"Oh, hi," she then said as he pressed himself against the wall.

"Hi," he responded to the pageboy haircut of Rebecca. "You performing as well?"

"For my sins. Which are many and varied," she added with a nervy laugh. "This is my first time."

"Me too."

Again that nervy laugh. "Oh God, I don't know about you but I'm wetting myself! You seem calm."

"The calmness of paralysis," Phil admitted.

For a few seconds they stood in awkward silence, not contributing to the surrounding clamour, then she asked, "When are you on?"

"No idea. How d'you find out?"

"Haven't you got a programme? There's a load by the door. And they're on the chairs. Here." She took one from the nearest seat and gave it to him.

Evans, written by *Ellis*, performed by *Ellis*, was fourth on the list. Suddenly, seeing the sketch title, seeing his name, he felt a dizzying sense of unreality. He was about to perform at the Footlights. Whatever the outcome, he would have performed at the Footlights. The *Footlights*. This moment couldn't be taken away from him. Ever. And what would be the outcome of it all? Would he permanently admitted to this hallowed haunt, or be permanently barred? Well, that was in the hands of God – or would be if he believed in God.

"That's me." He pointed at his entry on the programme. "Phil Ellis."

"I'm right after you." She in turn pointed to *The Taylor's Tale*. "I'm Rebecca – Rebecca Taylor. Not 'Becky'."

"Hi, not Becky."

She gave a tiny laugh and he wanted to say something more, anything, but the abrupt sound of a gong being repeatedly struck cut through the noise, and as the reverberations died down a hearty male voice cried out, "Ladies, gentlemen and undecided! Pray take your seats. The evening's entertainment will be unleashed on you in five minutes. Five minutes. Please take your seats."

They sat on the nearest available chairs, Phil taking from the pannier – before tucking it under the seat – a clipboard with script attached and a small handheld microphone from his tape recorder. People kept pushing past to other chairs beyond them, some of them then pushing back a minute or two later. Yelps and greetings and cries of recognition kept criss-crossing the room. Five minutes came and went. Ten minutes. On the stage the curtains were finally but sulkily closing, their shabbiness illuminated by floodlights. Next to him, Rebecca was talking with the other young woman who had been at the preliminary meeting.

Then the general noise in the room changed in quality to expectancy as the president mounted the few steps to the stage and held up a hand. "Good evening," he began. There came a cheer which he acknowledged with a brief bow. "Good evening," he repeated in a louder voice, and waited. Apart from bar sounds continuing from the far end and someone coughing, a near-silence now descended, but "Welcome, everyone, to the first smoker of the year!" elicited another cheer, another bow. "We have an excellent programme this evening," the president continued, "including a number of performers who are with us for the first time. Good luck to you in particular." He explained the process of the evening, pointing to a bench positioned against one wall and next to the little run of steps which led up to the stage. 'The agony bench', he called it. Performers, two items before they were due on stage, had to go and sit on it while waiting their turn. Three people already occupied it. Phil would have to join them after the very first item.

"And now, to start the proceedings," the president cried in conclusion, "I give you – and you can keep them! – 'les Palmas Moistas'!" He left the stage, and the curtains parted jerkily, revealing, to an enthusiastic reception, Bill the vice president and two others, who launched into a musical number which Phil recognised from the Edinburgh revue.

As the number ended and the applause started, Phil made his way to the agony bench, next to which stood a small table bearing jugs of water and glass tumblers. He helped himself and sat down next to a thickset young man wearing a top hat, attached to which was a phallic balloon in a state of extreme tumescence. For the next few minutes Phil remained oblivious to the content of what was happening on the stage, simply shifting along the bench when phallic balloon man, making his phallic balloon waggle, had shifted. Rebecca joined him. Then they shifted again as phallic balloon man disappeared up the steps and onto the stage. The noisy reception he received indicated that he was an old hand at this.

Phil would be next on. He drained his glass of water, but his mouth immediately felt dry again. When applause signalled the end of phallic balloon man's sketch, Phil dimly heard Rebecca telling him to break a leg. He stood up abruptly and stepped onto the lowest of the steps just as phallic balloon man started coming down them. As they almost collided, Phil felt himself treading on the other's foot before he became briefly flapped at by the curtain. He made it to the centre of the stage.

The lights dazzled. Only the first few rows of the audience were properly visible; the rest had merged into an indistinguishable mass. Deep breath. *Here goes.*

Stepping forward to the front edge of the stage, he raised to his mouth the little microphone, with its lead and jack plug dangling free, and began.

"Good evening, and welcome to *Match of the Day…*"

viii

The thunderous applause as he gave a quick bow and headed offstage astounded him. But the reception throughout the sketch had astounded him. The entire experience astounded him.

Admittedly the sketch had started slowly, with a few amused chuckles arising from the audience, suggesting a willingness to give him a chance without wanting to imply that he had yet been funny enough to provoke actual laughter – they had *chosen* to chuckle purely out of the goodness of their larynxes. Then had come the first proper laugh, one which they hadn't chosen to vocalise but which had caught them and their larynxes unawares: a spontaneous laugh when the football commentator, having identified four players in a row as being called 'Evans', referred to a fifth as 'Vladimir Kalshtock' before apologising and correcting himself for misreading the real name of 'Evans'. The big laugh had come exactly as the president, Adrian, had predicted.

A surge of confidence almost immediately led to another laugh. A few seconds later and an absolute belter of a laugh filled the room, lasting so long he had time to pause, gather his breath, take in the sight of the many-headed enjoying themselves, enjoying *him*. The exhilaration was immense, much like hurtling down a steep hill on a bike while refusing to apply the brakes.

The sketch continued with more good laughs, then another huge laugh, and another immediately following it, so that again, and then again almost immediately, he had to wait for the laughter to subside before continuing; until he came to the pay-off line, which elicited a massive cheer before giving way to the thunderous applause, and as he stumbled towards the wings, almost falling off the stage, he heard Rebecca, passing him as she went on, whisper, "Well done!"

Returning to his seat, he had someone slap him on the back and heard someone else hail him in a whisper, "Evans! Evans!" before giving him a double thumbs up. The other young woman, whom Rebecca had been talking with earlier, turned to give him a quick congratulatory smile across Rebecca's vacated seat.

Phil felt himself close to tears. His legs, he realised, were trembling. He couldn't think. Waves of some unnameable emotion kept sweeping through his body. He tried to listen to Rebecca delivering her lines but couldn't, though aware that she was garnering a decent number of laughs and, at her sketch's conclusion, generous applause. She looked pleased enough on returning to her seat.

The next performer performed. As did the next and the next...a double act, another musical item, a mime involving three people, a parody of *Peter and the Wolf*... He was now able to take note of what was happening on the stage, and yet again he was astounded: no one else appeared to elicit more than a couple of really big laughs, if that, whereas he had had to stop several times because of violent eruptions of laughter.

When the interval arrived, Rebecca turned to him and said, "That was some tour de force of yours!"

"It was all right, was it?" He forced into his voice a nonchalance he did not feel.

"All right? It was wonderful. *And* I reckon you got the audience into a great mood, so the rest of us benefited. I certainly did."

Phil discerned that she was probably hoping he'd say something in return in praise of her sketch, but he couldn't recall a single line from it. Best to come clean. "You went down well," he said, adding, "Look, really sorry, but I was still on a high. Didn't actually take in your sketch."

"No?" She looked disappointed for a moment, then laughed. "That's okay, I don't blame you. It wasn't really all that good, if truth be told."

"Bet it *was* good," said Phil, consciously being gallant.

"Maybe." She gave another laugh. "I guess I'll have to give you a private performance so you can decide for yourself."

For a moment they held each other's gaze.

"Name the time and place," Phil said. "But for now, name a drink!"

"Well done, Phil," Bill the vice president said, coming up to him with an extended hand. The entertainments had ended ten or fifteen minutes ago, and although some people had left, most were staying on and there was still a lively atmosphere. The honky-tonk pianist had resumed his impromptu recital, the bar was doing brisk business, various people were fooling about on the stage, and Phil himself was feeling exhausted. He took the proffered hand and asked as they shook, "When will I know?"

"Know what?"

"If I'll get in."

Bill pushed his spectacles up and stared at Phil. "Best jokes of the evening!" he said. "And Clive reckons it's the best sketch by a fresher he's ever seen."

"Clive?"

"Clive James."

"Bloody hell."

"So of course you'll get in. Take it from me, you're in. Good to have you."

"What about, um, Rebecca?" He nodded towards the bar, where she was getting more drinks.

"I expect so," Bill said. "I'll be voting for her, and I know Adrian rates her, but theoretically she won't know until the committee have met and had a chance to discuss all the newbies. That's tomorrow. But you're a dead cert."

Bloody hell, Phil repeated to himself as Bill moved off to speak with someone else. *I've made it. I've only gone and got myself into the Footlights. I've got into Cambridge, and now I've got into the Footlights!*

The euphoria of achievement stayed with him for weeks.

A Change of Mind

Graham Ferrari sometimes wore a beard and sometimes didn't. When he did, it tended to be bushy and splayed out. Then it started to itch, and after enduring the itching for a week or two he would shave it off. Regret would set in almost immediately, so that before long he would allow it to sprout again. And so it came and went.

He worked in the Research & Development section of Ace Biochemicals Corporation – ABC for short – which supplied laboratories throughout the world with esoteric products for the testing of medicinal drugs, pesticides, fertilisers, cosmetics and other chemical and biochemical essentials of modern existence. He had joined ABC straight from university, bringing to it all the benefits of his lower second. In his nine years there he had made, as a result of his researching and developing, a number of recommendations which had proved both scientifically and economically sound, and a few recommendations of opposite tendency. On balance he had been an asset to the company, but not so much so, he realised, that he was considered indispensable or that rival firms sought to lure him away with promises of astonishing facilities and fabulous sums of money. He had, to his regret, never been approached in pub or club by an industrial spy intent on extracting from him information about the company's latest biochemical brainchild. On some days he enjoyed his work and was thankful to be with congenial colleagues in a moderately well paid job; on other days he felt morose and hated work, and he'd leaf dispiritedly through the pages of scientific periodicals wondering if it were time to move on. But he never found the energy to send off for application forms.

Unmarried, he lived in a flat two or three miles from work. For five years he had been going round with a girl called Anne whom, he had vaguely supposed, he would one day marry. This vague supposition had become yet vaguer the previous summer when she had announced her intention of marrying an

Italian waiter she had met on holiday in Rome, and had vanished altogether on the day of the autumn wedding. Graham had not attended the wedding. He had not been invited. Since then, he had had no girlfriends; his only amorous adventure had been a brief dalliance with Rosemary from Accounts, and that had been at Christmas and had consisted of a drunken fumble in the back of a car. It did not really count. In the evenings he went to the pub for a drink with whomever happened to be there, or dropped in on Marc in the flat below, or stayed in to watch television. Sometimes, but not every week, he went along to the chess club – he had bursts of enthusiasm for the game.

One Wednesday evening in March he sat in his small sitting room hunched up over a chessboard, replaying a game which had taken place against Will Zakir during the lunch break. Will was his regular opponent at work: they were evenly matched. The television was on but Graham took no notice of it; the battle between black and white engrossed him entirely.

The buzzer sounded. Someone was wanting to be admitted to the block of flats. It had to sound again before he could drag himself away to answer it.

"Hullo?"

"Graham? Mr Ferrari? It's Julie here. Julie from work."

His head still full of forks and pins and other chess stratagems, Graham could not at first put a face to the name. Julie. Julie from work. *Was* there a Julie at work? Perhaps he had misheard.

"First floor," he said, pressing the button to release the main door. "To the right of the stairs."

He went to open the front door of the flat. A few seconds later a young woman appeared up the stairs from the ground floor. She wore a long, bright green and white coat made of shiny plastic, which creaked as she moved. She looked worried.

"Hullo there," Graham said, now recognising her as a new recruit to one of the Quality Control laboratories, just down the corridor from his own. She had been with ABC only a short time, and to date he had exchanged only a few sentences with her, all of them bearing on work. He could not imagine why she was calling on him.

"Oh, Mr Ferrari! Graham! I do hope you don't mind!" She was breathless, and her words came in short bursts. She shook her head and blinked rapidly, looking as though she were only just managing to hold back tears. Her coat made little creaking sounds of protest.

"Ah!" said Graham. He looked over her shoulder into the darkened passageway. He always intended to put on the light when it grew dark, and nearly always forgot. "Um, come in, Julie, come in. What are you doing in these parts? Or do you live nearby?"

"I hope you don't mind," she repeated, stepping into the tiny hallway as Graham moved to one side. He peered out into the passageway once more, then closed the door.

He directed her to the main room, where he replaced on the chessboard the black knight he had been clutching, carefully ensuring that it faced the white camp. The enemy camp. He was always very particular about that.

"Oh, chess," said Julie. "Of course, you play with what's-his-name at work. I've seen you in the canteen."

"Will," said Graham.

"Is that his name?"

"Yes. Will."

"He's foreign, though. Will isn't a foreign name."

"That's what he's known as. He did tell me his name, but it's pretty unpronounceable so he likes to be called Will. Will Zakir."

"Where's he from?"

"Shepherd's Bush."

"I mean originally."

"Somewhere in Pakistan. At least, I think that's where his parents live."

"What's he doing here?"

"Microbiological research. Same as you and me."

"Oh!" She gave a little, artificial laugh. A very young-girlish laugh. As she looked distractedly around the room, her coat again creaked in protest.

"Like a coffee?" asked Graham. "Or tea? Or a beer if you like. I have got some sherry, but it's not very nice. Too sweet."

"It's all right, thanks. I don't want anything. I won't bother you for long. I hope you don't mind me coming round like this."

"That's the third time you've said that."

"Well, I'd like to ask your advice, you see."

Graham blinked rapidly. A girl he hardly knew coming to ask his advice lay outside his daily experience. Way outside. He could conceive of no type of advice he could give – save, perhaps, concerning the optimal nutrient requirements of a wide range of microorganisms. Hardly the sort of stuff to warrant a surprise visit outside work hours.

"Sit down," he said. "What is it, then?"

The coat creaked.

"It's just that—"

"Here, shall I take your coat?" he interrupted. "Chuck it here. I'll hang it up. May as well be civilised."

"Oh, thanks."

She stood up again and removed her coat to reveal a white top and a short black skirt. She was also wearing what Graham assumed were tights, black tights – she didn't seem the type to wear stockings with such a short skirt. She sat down again and patted her hair. She had fair hair, cut short – almost an old-fashioned bob. He'd noticed before how attractive she was.

"To be honest," she said when Graham returned from hanging up the coat, "I haven't really got anyone who I can turn to. Not to confide in. I don't know many people down this way, and those that I do know at all well – I suppose I don't really want to tell them about it. In case – you know."

Graham didn't know, but refrained from saying so. He simply tried to look wise by nodding slowly and sucking in his cheeks.

"I thought – well, I get the impression you might be able to help," Julie continued. "You were very nice to me when I first came, and I feel sort of safe with you." She gave an embarrassed laugh and crossed her ankles. "I hope you don't mind me saying so?"

Graham unsucked his cheeks and gave an embarrassed laugh in his turn. He also crossed his ankles, noticing that she had crossed right over left, whereas he favoured left over right. Mirror images. Optical isomers.

"Not at all," he said. "Rather a compliment. But I didn't know I'd been particularly nice to you when you came. Was I?"

"Oh yes!" she nodded earnestly. "When I was being shown round. You made me feel at home."

Now Graham remembered. On her first day with the company, Julie, as was customary, had been taken round to the various departments she would have contact with and introduced to the staff. He'd just been informed that the recently successful completion of a long-term project had earned him an 'employee of the month' accolade, and he had been in a jovial mood, cracking some feeble jokes in her presence which, for some reason, she had found incredibly funny. This, presumably, constituted being nice to her.

"If you say so," he said. "That's nice to hear. Are you sure you don't want a cup of anything? I'm going to have some tea."

"All right, then. Thanks. No sugar."

He made some tea and brought it in with a selection of old biscuits he had disinterred from a slightly rusty tin. He munched his way through the entire collection as they talked. The ginger snaps were soft. Julie didn't have any of them.

"How long have you been at ABC?" she asked.

Graham considered, pausing mid-munch. "Several years. Too long, I sometimes think," he said in a fine spray of ginger biscuit. He brushed his pullover with his hand.

"Don't you like it, then?"

"It's all right. If you like that sort of thing. Which I do, from time to time. How about you?"

"I like it. I like it a lot. It's really interesting work."

"Good," said Graham. "That's good."

Julie put down her cup and stared at the chessboard, then tugged at the hem of her skirt as though suddenly worried that she was displaying something she ought not to be displaying. "What I wanted to ask you," she said slowly, "is sort of connected with work. Well, it is connected. You know John Woodley?"

"Uh-huh," Graham nodded. John Woodley worked in the larger of the two Quality Control labs, heading up the team there. He had joined ABC at the same time as Graham, though that had not led to any particular male bonding – an expression Graham always found amusing: were male bonds ionic or covalent? Or perhaps 'male bonds' were an as-yet-undiscovered form of atomic bonding. He had once considered writing a spoof article on the matter and submitting it to *New Scientist*, but had never got round to it.

"What do you think of him?" Julie asked, bringing Graham back to the present conversation.

"I don't really know him," he said – adding, as this appeared to contradict his previous assertion, "I mean, I know him in the 'hello John, hello Graham, how's things, not so bad, can I borrow three gross test tubes, sure help yourself' sort of way. But I don't know him any more than that, except that he likes to go sailing and has a yacht or some such down at Portsmouth or Plymouth or somewhere. I don't know the innermost secrets of his heart type of stuff. Why?"

"Well, it's just that he's been – well, how can I put it?" She shifted nervously in her chair and again tugged at the hem of her skirt. "He's been sort of getting interested, if you know what I mean, and—"

"Interested in you?"

"Yes. In me." She was looking away from Graham, as though the chessboard hypnotised her.

"Ah. In what sort of way?"

She now looked at him properly, moving her head, not just her eyes. "Well, I mean, he sort of keeps asking me to go out for a drink with him. Or a meal. Only he doesn't quite ask directly, but *implies* it, puts it forward as an idea that we should go out together."

Graham fiddled with his nascent beard. He isolated a stubbly hair and, gripping it between two fingernails, smartly plucked it out. The fleeting sharp sting was always strangely pleasurable, like squeezing a spot.

"And, er, have you?" he asked, examining his fingernails for the liberated hair, but it appeared to have fallen off.

"Oh no! No, we haven't!" She sounded shocked.

"And you don't want to?"

"That's the whole point. Yes, I do, in a way."

"Why don't you, then?"

Julie shrugged. "I don't know if I ought to, what with him still being married and everything."

Again she was not looking at Graham. She had started scratching the fingernails of one hand with the fingernails of the other. She had pretty hands – small and slightly dark. Graham's hands were also small, but pale, with several dull crimson splotches disfiguring them. Her fingernails were well manicured and trim, suitable for lab work; Graham wondered if she wore nail polish at weekends, away from the lab. His own nails were slightly dirty, some of them notched and cracked.

"I didn't know he was married," said Graham. "But then, why would I know?"

"They're separated. They've been separated for – well, I don't know how long. But Nick told me they're separated."

"Well, well, it just goes to show, doesn't it?" said Graham, though he realised as he said it that he didn't know what it went to show.

"And he keeps on implying that we should go out," Julie continued. "If he weren't married, I'd say yes, come on, let's go out. Even though he's obviously quite a bit older than me – but I do rather fancy him. And I'm wondering if it would be all right to? I mean, what with him being separated, that's like him being single, isn't it?"

"Single but married," said Graham.

"Yes."

"Unlike me – I'm single but single." He gave a brief snort of laughter.

"It's not as though I'd be taking him away from his wife, is it? Or breaking up his marriage," Julie continued. She had nice legs, Graham had decided. He was certain she had tights on, not stockings. Pity. He liked the idea of her sitting opposite him wearing stockings.

"But I might get in the way of any reconciliation," Julie was saying.

"Ah, good point. Is that a possibility? Reconciliation?"

Julie shrugged and uncrossed her ankles. "I can't tell. I don't know. He hasn't said." She sighed. "What do you think I ought to do?"

Graham didn't really think anything. He couldn't see that there was any problem, but it would not do to say so outright. For the girl it was obviously a great dilemma she found herself in, and it had to be treated as such. He shifted in his chair, then spent an inordinately long time rolling a thin cigarette he didn't really want. He found rolling cigarettes a soothing occupation, and a lot more satisfying than actually smoking them.

"Sorry," he said as he lit it. "Do you?"

"I won't, thanks."

"Wise." He drew on the roll-up. Its length diminished dramatically. He coughed.

"So, what do I think?" he said slowly, weighing each word carefully as though one of them contained a great philosophical truth, if only he could identify which one and decode it. "What do I think? What is it that stops you saying yes to John and going out with him? Just the fact that he's married?"

"I suppose so."

"Any kids?"

"I don't think so. No, I'm sure there aren't. It's just that I was brought up very strictly, and if I went out with him I'd feel terribly guilty."

"Moral scruples, eh?"

"Yes. The church I used to go to would really frown on it. Only I don't know if it really would be wrong, or if I would only *feel* it was wrong even if it wasn't. If you see what I mean."

"Yeah," said Graham. "An awful lot of crap is talked about morals, though."

"Do you think so?" She sounded earnest – eager even.

"I can't see that it's anyone's business but your own. If people want to say that this or that is wrong, let them."

"But I think I'd feel guilty, you see. I want to go out with John, but I don't want to feel guilty."

"Feeling guilty's got nothing to do with it really, in my opinion. I feel guilty every time I see a policeman, but that doesn't mean I've done anything wrong."

"That's exactly what I mean! So you think it would be all right for me to go out with him?"

Graham leaned forward and toyed with a white pawn. "Don't take my opinions for gospel," he said. "If going out with him would make you feel guilty and you find you can't stop feeling guilty, well, I don't know, but that might bugger up the relationship right from the word go. How old are you?"

"Twenty-two."

"There you are, then. You could have been married for years already. It's got to be your decision, but in my opinion there's no need to feel guilty. That's all."

Graham realised that he couldn't follow his own reasoning, but that didn't seem to matter.

"Do you think I could have a cigarette after all?" she asked. "I don't smoke much as a rule, only every now and again I feel in need of one."

"Sure."

He rolled her a cigarette, showing off by doing the actual rolling one-handed.

"That's clever," she said.

He rolled himself another, and they sat in silence, smoking. Graham liked the idea that the smoke from their two cigarettes mingled.

She stayed another ten minutes or so. They talked a little about work. Just as she was leaving, Graham asked how she had known where he lived.

"I asked Nick," she said.

"Oh, Nick," said Graham, nodding. Nick was his assistant in the lab. "I wonder how he knew. He's never been here."

"I'm sorry if I've messed up your evening."

"You haven't. I'm sorry I haven't been more helpful."

"Oh, you have!" Her plastic coat creaked as she leaned forward and kissed him on the cheek. "Honestly you have. I feel much better."

"Good," said Graham. "See you around at the gulag tomorrow."

Julie left. Graham returned to his sitting room, where he didn't continue with the chess.

*

110

Graham was in a good mood the next morning. He had never before considered himself the type to whom people turned for advice – mainly because never before *had* anyone turned to him for advice. Not of the emotional variety, at least. On reflection he reckoned he had handled the situation reasonably well. Not brilliantly, but at all events Julie had departed in a happier frame of mind. So he must have done some good.

Nick was late. He had been with ABC for eight months, during which time he had arrived punctually for the day's work a mere twice. Most mornings he rolled up about half an hour late; sometimes it was as much as an hour. Occasionally, if he was feeling morose, Graham would bawl his assistant out and threaten to report him to management; on other occasions he merely shrugged. His timekeeping apart, Nick was a good worker and genial company. He was twenty years old.

Graham was considering the implications of a graph relating microbial growth to nutrient concentration for a potential new product when Nick arrived. He was forty minutes late. His hair was tousled, his chin and cheeks unshaven, his eyes bleary.

"Good afternoon," said Graham.

"Hi there!" said Nick. He yawned, then blew his nose into a disgusting-looking tissue. "I feel like a coffee."

"You look like a wreck," said Graham.

"You want a coffee?"

"Go on then."

When Nick returned with two plastic cups of pale brown fluid, he looked at the graph Graham was still studying. "Anything exciting?"

"The overnight monitoring," said Graham.

"And? Any good?"

"Not bad. Quite promising actually."

Nick pulled up a stool and sat down heavily. He rested his feet on the desk and again yawned. He took the graph from Graham.

"That's good," he said. "Outperforms the previous what's-it."

What's-it, thought Graham. Not a very scientific term.

"And what's on the programme today?" Nick continued.

Graham outlined the next stage of the project, and Nick started to assemble the apparatus needed.

"You're in a cheerful mood," said Nick as Graham hummed to himself.

"And why not?" said Graham. "Work's going well. Nice results, nothing to complain of, no overdraft at the bank."

"On Monday you were looking for another job."

"On Monday it was Monday. Today's Wednesday."

"Thursday."

"Wednesday, Thursday, Friday – whatever it is, it isn't Monday. No, young Nick, I've no complaints. How about you?"

"I'm okay."

"No problems? Hang-ups? Little difficulties?"

Nick looked bemused. "No."

"You're managing life all right, then?"

"I reckon I'm having a fair crack at it."

"Well, I hope so. But if you ever do need a bit of help, don't hesitate to ask. You know where to come. Don't miss the opportunity of drawing upon my experience. Results guaranteed."

"Right," said Nick. "I'll remember." He sounded cautious.

Later that morning Graham had to go on the scrounge. Nick had dropped a vital piece of glassware. On his way back from the stores with a replacement piece, Graham paused at the small Quality Control lab and peered in. Julie was alone. In her white coat she looked neat and efficient. Two or three metal spatulas were protruding from her top pocket, and she was holding a plastic one in her hand. She was weighing out a white powder.

"Hello, Julie," said Graham.

She did not respond at first, intent on delicately tapping powder from the spatula onto a watch glass. The correct quantity measured, she looked up.

"Hello, Mr Ferrari."

"How are things? All right?"

Graham fancied she was startled by the question. "Yes, thank you," she said. "I'm just rechecking the latest batch. It seems to be too acid."

"You got back all right last night, then?"

"Sorry?"

"It struck me after you'd left last night that you might not know the quickest way. Actually, having said that, I don't even know where you live. Where do you live?"

"Whitmore Lane," she said. "Why?"

"Ah, I don't know it. Is it round here?"

"Not that far."

He was about to ask what number she lived at when John Woodley came up behind him.

"Mind out, Graham," he said, pushing his way past into the laboratory. He was carrying a sheaf of papers. "Julie, could you recheck yesterday morning's batch as well? There's another problem. I suspect the fail-safe has failed!" He pointed out something on one of the sheets of paper.

"All right, John," said Julie. "I'll do it in a tick."

"Doesn't matter," said Graham. "Another time."

Julie and John Woodley both looked up at him.

"About the…" Graham waggled his hand. "Not to worry."

"What was all that about?" he heard John Woodley ask as he returned along the corridor to his own laboratory.

At lunchtime he played chess with Will. All the encounters so far that week had gone Graham's way, but this time Will won.

"Good game," said Will as they packed the pieces away. "I thought you had me at one point – your rooks working well."

"So did I."

"I must study rook endings, though. Very weak."

"Stronger than me!"

"This time, perhaps."

"By the way," said Graham as he rolled himself a post-chess cigarette, "did you know John Woodley's separated?"

"Separated? What d'you mean?"

"From his wife."

"I didn't know he was married." Will had taken out a large white handkerchief and was mopping his face.

"Must be. But they've separated."

"I'm surprised." Will tucked his handkerchief back in his pocket. "He's a strong churchman – one of those house churches. Very strict, I thought. Sanctity of marriage and all that. He'll get drummed out."

"I suppose even churchgoers make lousy marriages sometimes," said Graham.

"Of course they do. I wonder what went wrong. Nice bloke, John."

"He's all right. Still, you never know. Dark horses and all that."

"What d'you mean?"

Graham considered. What *did* he mean? "I don't know," he said. "It's just a saying."

Will rose to his feet. "Right. Back to the bunsens," he said. It was his habitual phrase, though not a single old-fashioned bunsen burner existed in the building. "See you later at the meeting."

"Oh, the meeting," said Graham. "I was forgetting."

The meeting took place at three o'clock every first Thursday in the month to discuss the state of current projects and ideas for possible future projects. A variety of people were present that afternoon: Graham, Nick, Will, John Woodley, Julie, two representatives from Chemistry including another John, three from the larger Research & Development lab, and a manager called Mr Bridson, who chaired the meeting. Mr Bridson spoke the longest, but John Woodley and Graham were the most influential. Julie hardly spoke at all, and when she did it was to answer a question put to her, not make a suggestion.

After the meeting, Graham contrived to steer Julie onto one side. He had been trying to catch her eye for most of the meeting, but she had not responded.

"I'm sorry if I was a little obscure this morning," he said. "What had crossed my mind was that I could've run you home in the car, that's all."

"That's very kind of you," Julie said doubtfully. "But I get a lift from Sandra. She goes past my place."

Graham thought her dense. "I don't mean from work. I mean last night."

Julie swayed back from him as though he had bad breath. She had a small mole on the side of her nose which Graham had not noticed the previous evening.

"Last night?" she said. "I'm afraid you've lost me."

"When you came round," Graham said.

"I'm sorry," she said jerkily. "I really don't know what you're talking about. I was at home last night." Her eyes flicked about. "I must go. I've got to write something up before five."

She half-ran off, and caught up with John Woodley as he went through the doorway. Graham saw them talking together, and John Woodley paused to glance in his direction.

Frowning, Graham returned to his own laboratory.

*

iii

That evening he went to see Marc, who lived in the flat below. They drank beer. Marc played his guitar quietly, singing a song he had written.

"Like it?" he asked.

"Play it again," said Graham.

Marc played it again. It was good. An honest lyric, a melancholic tune. Graham marvelled that such sweet music could be produced by such an uncouth-looking person with such chubby fingers. He asked to hear it a third time, and when it was over Marc played several more of his own compositions. Graham had heard them all before, but never tired of them.

"I wish I could write stuff like that," he said. "I used to try scribbling poetry, but it came out all wrong. How do you do it?"

Marc scratched his beard. Long and straggly, it threatened to become entangled in the guitar strings whenever he played. But it never did.

"I don't try," he said. "If there's any secret, that's it. Don't try. If I try to write a song, I cock it up. I have to let the song write me."

"Ah," said Graham, not understanding. "I can't even write letters. Even the simplest ones make my mind go blank. I can never work out how to start them."

"Say what you've got to say, and when you've said it, shut up," said Marc, retuning his guitar strings. "Poetry, prose or music – it makes no difference."

"What if you don't know what you want to say?"

"In that case, don't say it."

"Ah," said Graham again. He understood that.

Marc slouched out into his kitchen to get more beer from the fridge. He was six feet tall with four-foot hair. While Marc was out of the room, Graham heard soft footsteps on the stairs outside. They went on up past Marc's flat, heading for the next floor. There came the faint ring of a doorbell. Graham thought it was his. He wondered who had let in the visitor through the main door.

The ring was repeated. Puzzled, he went to investigate, calling out to Marc, "I think I've got a visitor."

He found Julie standing outside his front door, her plastic coat creaking as she pressed the doorbell again. "Yes?" he said, meaning it to sound cold. He was annoyed with her.

Julie jerked round, her expression changing from concern to relief on seeing him. "Oh, good! I was afraid you weren't in, Graham."

"I'm not. I'm out."

"I don't know what I would have done if you hadn't been here," she continued. "I hope you don't mind. You don't, do you?"

Graham blinked. He thought he did mind.

"I don't get it," he said. "What's the point in coming back?"

"Oh no! You do mind!" Julie wailed. "Please don't be cross. But I must talk to you. Please."

Graham remembered how attractive she'd looked in her white lab coat. Feeling like a willing martyr, he let her into his flat before running downstairs to tell Marc.

"Can't stay. Someone's come to see me."

"Bring 'em down here. Plenty of beer."

"Rather private. Sorry and all that. Maybe see you later."

"Okay," Marc grinned. His thick pebble glasses gleamed faintly.

Graham went back to his flat, where Julie had gone through to the kitchen. Her coat lay on the floor.

"I'm making some tea," she called out. "Is that all right?"

"Sure. Fine." He did not really want tea himself on top of the beer, but didn't feel disposed to object. And if it made her happy...

Julie appeared with two mugs of tea. "It's not very tidy in there," she said. "Don't you ever do any washing-up?"

"Sometimes."

"It's not very hygienic."

"It's my system," explained Graham. "I wait until I've used up all the crockery and stuff, then I wash it all up in one go. Saves time. Don't have to use so much hot water or detergent either. Economical and ecological."

"That's the theory, is it?" said Julie. She was smiling. "You could get one of those slimline dishwashers."

"I could."

Julie sat in the same chair she had occupied the previous evening, and looked serious. She was wearing another short skirt – red this time. Her tights, if they were tights, were flesh-coloured.

"I'm sorry about today," she said. "I must have seemed awfully rude."

"Uh-huh?" said Graham, willing to be mollified.

"You took me by surprise, you see. I didn't want anyone to overhear, so I pretended I didn't know what you were talking about. I didn't want people to know what was going on."

"That explains it. I didn't think of that," said Graham, now definitely mollified. "No one would have overheard, though."

"I suppose not, but I got flustered. As it was, John wanted to know what it was all about."

"What did you tell him?"

"I said it was about work, that's all."

"Well, that's cleared that up," said Graham. "I'd begun to think you were playing some sort of practical joke on me, though I couldn't imagine why. You know, spin me a yarn and see how I'd react."

"Oh no!" Julie looked up abruptly and slopped tea from her mug onto the chair. She dabbed at it with a tissue. "I'm not joking or anything like that. Honest."

"Don't worry. I realise that now."

"Oh good." She leaned back in her chair and crossed her legs. Graham gazed at her thighs.

"I've got a confession to make, though," Julie said. "You see, I'm afraid I didn't tell you everything yesterday. I didn't want to make it any more complicated than necessary. But – well, I'd better tell you the position."

"Go ahead," said Graham. He pressed together the tips of his fingers and adopted an encouraging position.

"It's Gavin," said Julie.

"Who's Gavin?"

"I don't know quite what you'd call him. He's a sort of boyfriend, but more than a boyfriend. He's a sort of fiancé, only we're not engaged."

Graham raised an eyebrow. He wished he had the knack of raising his eyebrows singly, for that would allow him to express a wider and subtler range of astonishment and query. He had once spent some hours attempting to teach his eyebrows independence from each other, but the experiment, involving the copious use of adhesive tape, had been a failure. He had always been able to wiggle his ears independently, no training required, but his eyebrows always moved in unison.

"He doesn't live round here," Julie was explaining. "He lives back at home, where I come from, and I suppose I see him about once a fortnight or three weeks. He comes down here or I go home. We've been going out together for years."

"When are you planning to get married? Are you planning to get married?"

"That's the whole point. When indeed? We've sort of drifted into an engagement, only it's not a proper engagement. I haven't got a ring or anything.

I think we both assume we're going to get married sometime, but that's about it."

"It was like that with me once," said Graham. "A girl called Anne. We'd been going around together for five years and I reckoned that sooner or later we'd get hitched."

"Did you?"

"Do I look married?"

"Not if the kitchen is anything to go by. What happened?"

"She married someone else. Just like that. Mario. Or Dario. Italian, anyway."

"Weren't you terribly upset?"

Graham thought about it. "No, not *terribly*. Not after the first couple of days or so. A blow to the old ego and all that, but nothing more, really."

Julie sighed. "I think I'd feel the same way if Gavin and I split," she said. "I don't want to break it off with him, but if it did end I think I'd be relieved more than anything else."

"But you don't want to be the one who delivers the blow, is that it?"

"It must be. Yes."

Julie finished her tea and was running her forefinger round the rim of the mug as though trying to make it sing like a wine glass. When she then put the mug down on the floor, Graham could see even more of her thighs. Definitely tights, not stockings. After a moment's hesitation, he averted his eyes.

"So, what with Gavin on the one hand and John on the other," she added, "I'm in a right muddle."

"Has anything more happened on the John front?" Graham asked. "Anything since yesterday, I mean? I suppose there hasn't been time."

"Oh, there's been time all right. I – I really don't know how to react. You know after the meeting I said I had some results to write up? Well, I was sitting in the lab at the desk, working out some things, and he came in."

She glanced down, and apparently noticing the amount of leg on display she tugged modestly at her skirt.

"What happened?" said Graham. "Did he say something?" He hoped it wasn't anything too innocuous.

"It wasn't what he said," said Julie, still looking down. "It was what he did."

"What was that, then?"

"Well, he came up to me and put his arms round me. From behind."

"And hugged you?"

"More than that. He gave me a squeeze. Up here. My boobs."

She had a good figure. Graham could believe that she would be well

118

worth fondling, even through the thick sweater she was wearing this evening.

"Anything else?" Graham asked hopefully.

"That was all."

"Did you tell him to stop it?"

Julie wriggled uncomfortably on the chair. "Well, yes, I suppose I did. I mean, I did tell him to stop, but not right away. To be honest, I rather enjoyed it. He's got nice hands. But it made me feel awfully guilty."

She was still not looking at Graham. Her hands were rhythmically clenching and relaxing, as though she were squeezing those rubber balls for improving muscle strength.

"I don't know what you must think of me," she said. Graham could hardly catch her words. "It must sound like I'm a dreadful flirt."

"Hmm," said Graham. He could not decide what she wanted him to say. Non-committal noises seemed the safest response.

They sat in silence.

Graham rolled them both a cigarette. "You said yesterday that you'd feel guilty if you went out with John. Would you feel so guilty if this Gavin fellow wasn't hanging around?"

"Probably not. You see, I don't want to let Gavin down. I don't want to be unfair to him."

"But you'd rather be shot of him in any case? Suppose John didn't exist – how would you feel about Gavin then?"

"I still wouldn't want to marry him," said Julie. "It wouldn't work. I think we go out together because we've always gone out together. It's that sort of relationship."

There was another silence. Julie broke it by heaving one of her sighs.

"What's that about?" asked Graham.

"I'm going to end it with Gavin. I have to, don't I? What's happening with John has precipitated things. Made me realise."

"Sounds like a good idea."

"There's only one problem, though." Julie's voice, which had risen in determination, dropped again. "How do I tell him? He'll go up the wall. He's got quite a temper."

"Can't you just write to him?"

"I suppose I could. But knowing him he'd come straight here and we'd have a terrible row. I wouldn't stand a chance."

Graham had a fleeting vision of himself as a knight on a white charger.

"If there's any trouble on that score," he said, "you know where to find me."

"Would you help? Give me moral support? That'd make all the difference, it really would. I don't know how I can thank you."

Her skirt was riding up again; her thighs were once more well on show.

"Right," said Graham. "And when we've got the Gavin problem settled, we'll be in more of a position to work out what to do about John. Yes or no, that sort of thing."

"I think you're right. It's ever so good of you. I really am grateful."

"All part of the service."

There was nothing more to say. Graham stared vacantly out of the window. He hadn't drawn the curtains. It was very dark outside. From below came the occasional sound of Marc's guitar. He couldn't hear him singing.

"He plays a lot," said Graham. "He's a good guitarist. Writes his own stuff."

"Do you play?"

"I'm not musical."

"Nor me," said Julie. "In fact, I'm not much good at anything. Are you good at chess?" She picked up the white bishop from the board. Graham reached out and took it from her, stroking it lovingly.

"Reasonable," he said.

Julie stood up and smoothed down her skirt. "I'd better be going."

"Do you want a lift?"

"I won't, thanks. I like walking. It helps me think." She retrieved her coat.

"And you're going to write to Gavin, aren't you?"

"I've got to. And if I have any difficulty with it, I'll come running!"

"You do that."

They were at the front door. Graham opened it.

"Thanks again," said Julie, and quickly kissed him.

Graham followed her down the flight of stairs and opened the main door for her. She went out into the street, turned and gave a little wave, and walked into the dark. Graham watched as she passed under one street light, then he closed the door and returned to Marc's flat.

Marc had put his guitar to one side and was doing something with the second-hand harmonium he had recently acquired.

"It's got a good tone," he said, furiously pumping the foot pedals and holding down several keys. An end-of-the-pier sound filled the room. "I'll plague you with it in the small hours."

"It's nice."

"Your visitor gone?"

"Yes."

"Of the female variety?"

"Yes again. Girl from work."

"Can be tricky, office romances."

"It's not a romance," said Graham. "And I don't work in an office."

"Laboratory romance," said Marc. "Test-tube babies." He played a brief tune on the instrument. It wheezed and groaned on some of the notes.

"You'll need a monkey to collect the money," said Graham.

"You'll do."

With his long hair, straggly beard and unkempt clothes, Marc looked like a leftover from the hippy era. He was doing postgraduate research on the subject of the moral ethos of the nineteenth century as portrayed by minor novelists.

Graham liked him. He was a gentle person.

iv

"I don't know who your informant is," said Will Zakir, "but whoever it is, they're wrong."

"My turn for black," said Graham. "Who's wrong?"

"Whoever told you that John Woodley's separated. He can't be – he's not even married."

"How do you know?"

"I was talking to Sandra this morning. She's known him for years, outside work. Anyway, John was mentioned for some reason, so I asked her."

"And?"

"She said he's a confirmed bachelor."

"Gay?"

"Couldn't say. She didn't say so."

"You're quite sure?"

"Well, old man, you can always ask Sandra herself if it matters that much to you." Will sounded nettled. "Or why not challenge John outright if you want to? 'I say, Woodley, I've discovered your little secret. Leave the money in the middle cubicle of the men's bog by Thursday lunchtime or you'll be for it.'"

Graham dismissed Will's facetiousness with a wave of his hand. He was now more concerned with avenging yesterday's defeat. They were sitting at their usual table in the canteen, the chessboard set up between them. Will pushed forward his queen's pawn, and no more was said on the subject of John Woodley.

Part way through the game, Julie entered the canteen, accompanied by Sandra. Graham tried to attract her attention in order to give her a conspiratorial wink, but she ignored him. As a result, Graham lost his concentration and a knight. A few moves later, Graham's position was hopeless. He knocked over his king in resignation and held out a congratulatory hand.

"Your mind was on other things," said Will, smiling. "Right, back to the bunsens."

During the afternoon, Nick surprised Graham. "What's all this about you and Julie?" he smirked.

"What do you mean?"

"Oh, just the rumour of a rumour, but I gather you've got your eye on her, eh?"

"Oh God," said Graham, "things do get distorted. Just because she asked you where I live, you jump to all sorts of conclusions."

Nick looked puzzled. "No," he said. "She's not said anything to me. I don't really know her."

"What are you going on about, then? 'Rumour of a rumour'?"

Nick spread his arms in an exaggerated gesture of ignorance and knocked a conical flask onto the floor. It shattered.

"Nothing really," he said, scuffing the fragments into a heap with his shoe. "All that happened was that Mike overheard Julie saying something to John – John Woodley, not the other John – about you, and Mike wondered if I knew anything. Is there anything between you two?"

"No, there isn't. Nothing at all. There is nothing going on between me and Julie."

"'The lady doth protest too much, methinks'!"

"Go and get the dustpan and brush and sweep that lot up, will you?"

"Okay, okay, don't get your DNA in a twist. Here, what do you call an item of laboratory glassware with an IQ of 150? A smart retort!"

When Nick returned and was engaged in sweeping up the remnants of the flask, Graham said, "You mean Julie didn't ask you for my address?"

"Why the hell should she? And I don't even know your address."

"She told me she'd asked you."

"She must have been thinking of two other people. She's never mentioned you to me. Why should she? You're not exactly a riveting topic for conversation."

"How well do you know her?"

"I told you," said Nick, tipping the fragments into the bin, "I don't. Mind, I wouldn't mind getting to know her a bit better. Great pair of legs. I'm a legs man. What about you?"

"She definitely told me you'd given her my address," persisted Graham.

"So there *is* something going on?"

"Not what you're thinking."

"What, then?"

"Mind your own business. And out of the way – I want something from that drawer."

"Yessir!" Nick sprang to attention, threw a mock salute and knocked a retort off the workbench.

Graham left work early, pleading a headache. Marc was in. With him was his newly acquired girlfriend, Claudine. A large woman with an angular face and a strident voice. She insisted on singing what she claimed were Swedish love songs, accompanied by Marc on the harmonium. They sounded more like dirges, as she wheezed and groaned more than the instrument. Her body vibrated with passion, her voice damaged eardrums at a hundred paces, the lyrics were incomprehensible. The total effect was vile. Graham had met her twice before but was still not convinced of her existence: how could such a person be? When her songs had finished, she launched into a diatribe against the philosophy of Spinoza. Why Spinoza? Graham wondered. What had Spinoza ever done to her? His admission, in reply to a brusque demand, that he had never opened a work of philosophy of any kind elicited from her a theatrical sneer. Marc smiled benignly.

She left early in the evening to attend a meeting demanding the overthrow of governments. Not *the* government, but governments.

"What do you see in her?" asked Graham.

"She's all right," said Marc. "She interprets songs well."

"They need interpreting."

"And she has her qualities."

All of them bad, thought Graham. "Full of herself," he remarked.

"That's Claudine for you. I know she's not everyone's cup of crème de menthe, but I like her."

"Swedish songs and all?"

"Swedish songs and all. You're back early," he added.

"Bit pissed off at work."

"Now then, my friend, I have just the antidote for that. Claudine has acquired some stuff for me, guaranteed to banish all pissed-offness."

A couple of weeks earlier, they had had a conversation about drugs. Graham had never indulged, and Marc had promised to get hold of some hash.

Marc fashioned a misshapen cigarette from three cigarette papers and some loose tobacco, into which he crumbled a small piece of a greenish substance. He gave a final twist to the end of the cylinder and lit up. He inhaled two or three times then handed it over to Graham. Graham was nervous. After two lungfuls he went dizzy, felt cold and sweaty and started to panic. His eyesight blurred and began to break up into little white patches, like a jigsaw puzzle.

"Relax," said Marc. "Just put your head between your knees. You'll be fine."

The dizziness passed, the cold sweat receded, his eyesight cleared. Graham began to enjoy it. They continued to smoke. Marc was lying on the floor, cradling his guitar, plucking the strings. The notes detached themselves from the strings and formed shimmering globules which floated away in endless succession. They ranged in colour: green, blue, red, lilac, and other hues which did not normally exist. Very intense. Very pure. Graham reached out to grasp the notes as they floated by, but they eluded him. His hands passed through them. Giggling, he rose unsteadily to his feet and stumbled round the room in pursuit of the shimmering notes. More and more flooded from the guitar, like soap bubbles on a windy day. They filled the room.

Then Marc stopped playing. The notes ceased to shimmer, but rose in a body to the ceiling, which they passed through and out of sight. Graham sat down again, still giggling.

"Let's go out," suggested Marc an indefinite time later. They headed for the park and climbed in over the gate. Shadows lurked.

"Look at the moon," said Marc.

"It's grinning at me," said Graham. It was a new moon, a thin, lopsided grin.

"Grin, grin, grin," said Marc.

"Grin, grin, grin," echoed Graham.

"A moonbeam smiles on us."

"Smile on, moonbeam."

The trees were swaying – not only their branches but their entire trunks as well. Great sinuous waves of arboreal motion. Undulating. Graham lay down on the grass and stared up at the sky. Few stars were visible. Marc was capering about, quietly whooping.

They played on the children's swings, the see-saw and the slide. The slide was by far the best. The journey from top to bottom never ended. They both decided against going on the roundabout.

As they left the park, climbing back over the gate, a huge, green, amorphous thing stalked Graham. He couldn't see it, but he knew it was there: like all huge, green and amorphous things, it was huge, and green, and amorphous. Two or three times he turned round sharply, confident of catching it out, but despite its great size it moved with great speed, slipping into the shadows or behind his back. He didn't mention it to Marc: it was *his* huge, green, amorphous thing.

They returned to Marc's room and drank coffee. It didn't taste like coffee. There was a buzzing in Graham's head inserted, he knew, by the huge, green, amorphous thing. He fell asleep to the sound of the guitar.

When he awoke, he stumbled back upstairs to his own flat and went to bed without undressing. Marc he had left asleep on the floor, cradling his guitar.

v

Nothing happened over the weekend. Claudine was staying with Marc, so Graham kept his distance. Dirgeful Swedish love songs filtered up to him with monotonous regularity. On Saturday he drove over to his brother's and spent a tedious time discussing gardening. Graham loathed gardening. Brian and Amanda loved it. He had nothing else in common with his brother. On Sunday he washed his car, topped up the oil, checked the brake and clutch fluids, adjusted the plugs and points. On his way to work the next morning the fan belt broke. He arrived twenty minutes late and Nick, punctual for only the third time, smirked at him.

At lunchtime he had no one to play chess with. Will was on a week's leave. Graham sat at their usual table in the canteen, feeling at a loss. He had in the past occasionally played with the other John, but he wasn't in either. He was about to go when John Woodley joined him.

"Mind if I sit here?" John Woodley asked.

"Go ahead."

John Woodley sat down awkwardly and pulled his chair close to the table. He looked in danger of crushing himself.

"I'd like a word with you, Graham," he said abruptly, leaning forward until his forehead was within an inch of Graham's. Graham raised his eyebrows – if only he had been able to raise just the one, it would have looked so much more interrogative. As it was, he had to supplement the action with words.

"What about?"

John Woodley cleared his throat. It was not a pleasant sound. "It's a serious matter."

"Still got problems with the pH levels?"

"Not at all," said John Woodley. "It's nothing like that. I'm here as an intermediary. I've been asked to have a word with you on someone else's behalf, man to…er…"

"Man?" suggested Graham.

"Man," John Woodley agreed. "You might think this is none of my business, and in a certain sense you would be right – it would be none of my business if it weren't taking place on company property during work hours, *and* if I hadn't been asked to intercede. But it is and I have, so it has become my business, if you follow me."

Graham didn't, but he nodded.

"It concerns Julie Grant," continued John Woodley.

"Aha," said Graham. He leaned back in his chair. This should be interesting. "Young Julie, eh?"

"Miss Grant tells me, and I have no reason to doubt her word and every reason to believe it, that you have been showing an interest in her recently, in an amatory manner."

"An amateur manner?"

"Making advances to her – advances which are not welcome. I understand that she has attempted to ignore them, but you have refused to take the hint. As I am her immediate senior she has quite rightly confided in me, and I said that with her permission I would have a word with you."

"Now, hold on—" began Graham.

"There's too much sexual harassment in the workplace these days," continued John Woodley, faltering slightly over which syllable to stress in the word 'harassment'. "And I must say I think it's a bit thick, a man like you chasing

126

a girl who must be ten or eleven years younger than yourself – she's only nineteen."

"She's twenty-two."

"Nineteen. But that's not relevant. What is relevant is that you're putting her in an extremely embarrassing position. Naturally she doesn't want to create trouble, but neither does she want your sort chasing after her."

Graham had started to roll a cigarette, but the tobacco spilled off the paper. He abandoned the task.

"You're talking a load of crap, John," he said. "And I reckon you've got a hell of a bloody nerve coming along here and trying—"

"I have her permission and I see it as my duty," John Woodley interrupted. "Not a pleasant task, but it had to be said. I trust you'll accept it in the right spirit and stop hassling her."

"Now look here," Graham started, but John Woodley had extricated himself from his chair and was walking away. Graham picked up a dinner knife and jabbed it into the tabletop. A canteen supervisor remonstrated with him.

At ten o'clock that evening, Julie appeared. She had clearly been crying.

"Now what are you up to?" Graham demanded.

"It's Gavin."

"I'm not interested in Gavin. I don't give a toss about Gavin. What stories have you been spinning to John Woodley?"

Julie's eyes opened wide. "Why? What's he been saying?"

Graham glowered at her. "You'd better come in," he said ungraciously.

They went into the main room, where Graham stood with his hands on his hips, facing her. "Do you want to know what happened?" he demanded. "He tried warning me off you."

"What do you mean? He can't have."

"But he did. You've been telling him that I've made advances to you, and that you're fed up with it or some such rubbish."

"No! That's all wrong! I did talk to him about you, yes, but it wasn't like that. Honestly."

"What was it like, then?"

"Can I sit down, please?"

Graham considered. "Yes. All right."

Julie slipped off her coat, and they sat in the same chairs as before. She looked woebegone.

"Come on, then," said Graham.

"It's just that I wanted to cool him off," said Julie helplessly. "I decided that whatever happened about Gavin, it still wouldn't be right to get involved with John, so I wanted to stop it right away. So I told him that I'm going out with you. You don't mind, do you? I'm sorry, I should have asked you first. I didn't think it would cause you trouble with him. I didn't actually say we're going out together, just that we'd been seeing a lot of each other recently. Which is true, isn't it?"

Graham thought of her thighs and agreed.

"I thought," she continued, "that if he believed you were my...well, my..." She paused, stumbled over the words and came to a confused halt.

"You thought that if he believed I was your boyfriend, he'd stop trying it on with you?" supplied Graham.

"That's right. Something like that."

"Oh," said Graham, subdued. "I see. It doesn't quite seem to have worked, though. All that's happened is that he now sees me as a rival to be warned off."

"Oh dear," said Julie. "I am sorry. Are you cross?"

"Not now," said Graham. "I can handle him. The main thing is that we've cleared up the misunderstanding between us."

"Good," said Julie, and smiled. Then Graham remembered something else.

"Here," he said, "didn't you say you'd got my address from Nick?"

"That's right."

"He doesn't know anything about it."

"I expect he forgot."

"But he doesn't even know this address."

"Doesn't he? He must have looked it up for me. No, I remember, I did ask him, but you're right, he didn't know, and suggested I ask Personnel. That's where I got it from. Sandra did me a favour."

"How well do you know Nick?"

"I've known him for ages. He was the one who told me a vacancy was coming up here. That's why I applied for the job."

"But he says he doesn't know you at all."

"What is this?" Julie wailed. "A cross-examination? Why should I know why Nick said that? He was probably fooling about. He's always fooling about. He's got a strange sense of humour."

That's true, thought Graham.

Julie was still wailing. "I came for your help, Graham. Please don't be like this."

Swedish love songs were again in evidence from below. Claudine appeared to have moved in permanently with Marc. Julie's sobs continued, and Graham relented. He went to make some coffee this time, not tea.

"Let's get something clear," he said on his return. "I'm no agony aunt. I can't untangle love lives. I'll help if I can, but don't expect miracles."

Julie's tears had increased. Graham glanced fearfully at the door, expecting that at any moment people would rush in demanding to know what all the noise was about. Perhaps he was still being too hard on her.

"I haven't got anyone else to turn to," Julie was saying between sobs. "I just need someone I can talk to about it all. I'm not asking for miracles. I came round because of Gavin, and now you're saying you're not interested."

"I've just said I'll help if I can. I *am* interested. Look, have some of the coffee, then tell me what it is about Gavin you want to say."

Julie sipped at her coffee. When she was a little calmer, she said, "I wrote to him. I told him I thought it would be best if we stopped seeing each other as it wasn't really working. I didn't put anything nasty in the letter – I tried to be nice about it."

"Yes," said Graham. "That sounds good. Well done."

"Anyway, he rang me this evening. About an hour ago. He was in a terrible mood – told me I was being a stupid little girl and manipulative and things like that. He just went on and on."

"Nasty," said Graham. "What happened in the end?"

"Oh, I tried to reason with him, I tried to make him see my point of view. I said I'd talked it over with a friend—"

"Did you mention my name?" asked Graham, feeling uneasy.

"No, I just sort of said a friend. I implied it was a girl friend. Sandra. But he wouldn't take any notice, and in the end I got so angry I cut him off. He rang again immediately – but I wasn't going to talk to him, so I didn't answer. But it's gone and left me feeling awfully guilty. That's why I had to come and see you again."

"I see," said Graham. Cigarette-rolling time had arrived. "He can't force you to stick with him," he continued when the cigarette had been manufactured and lit. Julie had turned down the offer of one.

"I'm worried, though," she said. "What if he comes down here to have it out with me? What do I do then? I can't stand a big argument, face to face – I'd just cave in."

"Maybe you should move out for the time being," Graham said. "Move in with a friend, but don't tell him where."

"Yes, I suppose I could, couldn't I?"

"Yes, you could."

"That's a really good idea."

Julie was leaning back in her chair, and looked reflective. Graham continued smoking his cigarette. After a while she said, "You're very reassuring. I mean, I feel much better just coming to see you."

They did not talk any more on the subject. Graham put an album on and their conversation turned to musical tastes. They both liked soft rock.

"I'll run you back," Graham said when the album had finished.

"It's all right, there's no need."

"No, I will."

"All right. Thanks."

Julie directed him to Whitmore Lane. It was not all that far. She occupied a ground-floor bedsit.

"D'you want to come in?" she said.

Her room was small, with not much furniture. She sat on a hearthrug in front of a decrepit gas fire, which popped and gurgled and glowed unevenly. She leaned back against a small armchair in an attitude of weariness, while Graham sat on the bed. They each had a glass of white wine. After a while Julie rose to her feet and left the room. When she returned she sat on the bed next to Graham, pressing up against him. He put his arm round her, and a few seconds later they were kissing. Her skirt had ridden up her legs, with Graham's hand following. Since they were on the bed it was only natural to lean back and then, by swivelling their bodies, to lie back.

Julie's tights were soon discarded onto the floor, joining Graham's trousers. A minute or so later her lacy yellow knickers and his plain blue underpants followed. Julie gurgled like the gas fire and clung tightly to him. Soon Graham was in a position to push home his advantage.

vi

Graham awoke. Julie was still asleep beside him, pressed against him in the single bed. He wasn't sure he had intended making love with her, but was not sorry it had happened. Quite the opposite. He wondered if she had intended it.

He eased himself out of the bed. Julie stirred, muttered something incomprehensible, and seemed to return to a deep sleep. She looked young and sweet.

He dressed as quickly and as quietly as he could. He took a piece of scrap paper from a waste bin, wrote *Graham x x* on it, and placed it next to the kettle. He let himself out. In the hallway was a payphone; he put its number in his mobile.

The next day, Tuesday, he did not go into work. He phoned up at eleven to say he had been taken ill. In a way, this was true. He did not feel guilty about taking time off for an imaginary illness; several times over the years he had struggled into work despite feeling under the weather. This partly redressed the balance. Besides, there had never seemed any point in taking time off for illness; far more logical to take time off for health.

Sun and showers alternated as he wandered down to the park – the same one he and Marc had climbed over the gate of a few evenings ago. Some children were playing on the swings and slides, watched by a small group of women and one or two men. He spent a few minutes following the fortunes of a lone golfer on the pitch-and-putt. Six old men in flat white caps were playing bowls on the bowling green. A mechanic whistled as he tinkered with a grass-cutting machine. Graham ignored him.

He wandered back, buying a newspaper on the way. As he reached the entrance to the block of flats, Claudine – she of the Swedish love songs – appeared from the opposite direction. She strode along, brandishing a sheaf of papers.

"Slavic dirges," she announced. Her voice echoed off the buildings on the other side of the road. "Tremendously expressive. I found them in the junk shop. You must come and listen to me playing them."

Graham knew the junk shop she meant. He had bought most of his furniture there. It was junk.

Slavic dirges? If Swedish love songs emerged from Claudine's vocal cords sounding like dirges, what would Slavic dirges sound like? Graham did not wish to find out. He started to say so, but Claudine had not invited or suggested. She had commanded.

"All right," said Graham.

They went into Marc's flat. Marc was out. Claudine sat at the harmonium and placed one of her finds on the music rest. With a technique not entirely suitable for the instrument, she thumped away. The notes had no chance to be born before being strangled. Her feet did not pump the pedals evenly, and the sound waxed and waned erratically. It had the air less of a dirge than of seedy joviality, until she began to sing. It sounded deadly enough then.

"I really must have another hunt through that shop," she announced, having played all eleven dirges. "I told the man to put aside any more that came his way."

Graham yawned. He had picked up Marc's guitar and was trying to remember the three chords he had once been shown. He became aware of Claudine staring at him.

"I fancy a good romp in a double bed," she stated.

Graham eyed the door.

"Much better now than at night," she continued. "More energy." She had already taken off her top garment to reveal an overfull bra.

Graham clutched the guitar in front of him for protection. "I don't think it's on," he said.

Claudine paused in the middle of unleashing her breasts. "Are you gay?"

"No."

"Then what's stopping you?" She took a pace towards him, her bra falling to the floor. Graham, who had stood up, tried to take a pace backwards and nearly fell over a chair. "I don't mind if you are gay," said Claudine.

"I'm not in the mood," said Graham.

"I'll soon change that." She was pulling down her jeans and knickers. "I'm a good lay. You won't regret it."

"I've given it up for Lent," Graham said.

"Please yourself. If you change your mind any time, though, just let me know. I'm always up for a romp."

Graham left. He went and bought lunch in a café, then spent the afternoon in the library. On returning to his flat, he found that some joker had tipped salt everywhere. Not just the occasional grain but whole masses of it. His sitting room looked like the Arctic: great drifts of the stuff. Carpet, chairs, table, stereo: everything covered in salt. It was the same in the bedroom, kitchen and bathroom. It lay an inch or two thick throughout the entire flat. Masses of salt.

With a soft-bristled brush he ineffectually tried to sweep it up, but abandoned the attempt after a few minutes and went to borrow a vacuum cleaner from a neighbour on Marc's floor. His one was broken.

It took ages to clear the flat of salt. Each time the vacuum was full, he emptied its contents down the lavatory and flushed it away. Salt still lurked in odd corners, crunched under his feet, flew up in his face when he sat down.

When returning the vacuum cleaner, he passed Claudine on the stairs. He stopped, wishing to interrogate her, but she looked at him enigmatically and passed by, saying nothing.

"Why salt?" he called out after her.

That evening he phoned Julie. He thought she wouldn't answer – who uses a payphone these days? – but he didn't have her mobile number. To his surprise, just as he was going to ring off, the phone was answered. It was Julie herself.

"Can I come round?" he asked.

"Why?"

"We ought to have a talk."

"What about?"

"Things. Us. After last night. I've been off work today."

"So have I," said Julie. "You don't mind about last night, do you?"

"I enjoyed it," said Graham.

"So did I. But I hadn't planned it that way, honest."

"What makes you think that I might have thought you had?"

"I'm not sure. I think I just thought you might think that I'd thought that."

The thinks and thoughts were becoming too complex. Graham rang off, having said he would be round in half an hour.

When he arrived in Whitmore Lane, no one was there. He waited twenty minutes but Julie didn't return. He left his car where it was and wandered off along the street. A drizzling rain fell. He came to a pub called the Lamb and Flag, where it appeared that live folk music was on offer, and went inside.

With a pint of beer in his hand he lounged against the wall, listening to the musicians. Several of them were rather good, the audience appreciative. Then a large woman with a determined chin took the floor, announcing her intention of singing a number of Swedish love songs.

"Bloody hell!" said Graham loudly. At that moment a collective silence had fallen, and his utterance sounded out clearly. Everyone turned to look at him.

Claudine's operatic-manqué voice arose and entertained the clientele for ten minutes. She received the longest and loudest ovation so far accorded to anyone, and an encore followed of Slavic dirges. When Graham pushed his way to the bar to get a second refill, he ran into Nick.

"I thought you were ill," said Nick.

"I am now," said Graham.

"You don't look it."

"I'll be back tomorrow. What do you make of this racket?"

"Brilliant," said Nick.

"You're joking."

"You made a right pillock of yourself," said Nick, "shouting out like that when she started. It was you, wasn't it?"

"Constructive criticism," said Graham.

"Constructive bullshit," said Nick. "Here, want a pint?"

Claudine had been replaced by Marc, who played two of his own songs which Graham thought marvellous. He applauded enthusiastically.

"Crap," said Nick.

"Great stuff," said Graham.

"Crap, I tell you. He's played here before. Never been any good. Same old self-indulgent hippy crap."

"You come here regularly?"

"On Tuesday. Tuesday night is music night. Or crap night, if he's playing."

"Ah."

"But this isn't your usual stamping ground, is it? What are you doing in these parts?"

"Just looking."

When he left the pub, Graham returned to Julie's. This time she was in. She opened the door only part way.

"Hello," she said. "Oh, Mr Ferrari!" There was surprise in her voice.

"Where have you been?" asked Graham.

"What? When?"

"This evening."

"I've been out. I've only just got back. Why? Why do you want to know? What are you doing here?"

"Why didn't you stay in?"

She blinked several times. "I don't like staying in. Why should I?"

"But you knew I was coming round."

"I didn't know that. How could I have?"

"You did! I'd said so. Look, can I come in?"

Julie hesitated and glanced behind her. Graham got the impression she wasn't alone.

"It's a bit late," she said.

"Be like that," said Graham. He turned and walked away. There came the sound of a front door being slammed shut.

He drove home. Some joker had tipped sand everywhere. Not just the occasional grain but whole masses of it. His sitting room looked like the Sahara: great drifts of the stuff. Carpet, chairs, table, stereo: everything covered in sand. It was the same in the bedroom, kitchen and bathroom. It lay an inch or two thick throughout the entire flat. Masses of sand.

It was too late at night to go and borrow the vacuum cleaner a second time. He made a drink, first having to empty sand from the kettle, then went to bed.

The sand was between the sheets. It irritated him all night.

vii

Graham returned to work the next day. Nick did not come in at all. At the beginning of the lunch hour, as he was heading for the canteen, he was collared by John Woodley and hustled along a corridor to the end door, marked *EMERGENCY EXIT: KEEP CLEAR AT ALL TIMES*. The door was padlocked for security reasons.

"See here, Ferrari," John Woodley was spluttering. "We've all had more than enough of you!"

Graham had also been spluttering. "Oi! Oi! Oi! Oi!" he now said meaninglessly.

"I told you before about Miss Grant!" John Woodley wagged a finger an inch from Graham's nose. His tie, normally secured by a large Windsor knot, was awry. "But just in case it didn't sink in, I'm going to spell it out to you once and for all. Lay off her! Got it? Lay off!"

"Lay off?" said Graham. "I reckon—"

"It's lucky for you you weren't in yesterday," John Woodley continued. "When Julie told me you'd been continuing to pester her I could have – I could have…" His spluttering got the better of him. Spittle was flying out of his mouth.

Graham wiped his face. "I think you ought to mind your own business," he said calmly. Unable to move his eyebrows independently, he resorted to waggling his left ear.

"It is my business!" John Woodley was going red in the face, a phenomenon

135

Graham had never before observed at such close quarters. "Miss Grant has specifically – I repeat, specifically – requested me to intervene on her behalf. Do you understand? When she informed me yesterday—"

"She wasn't at work yesterday," Graham interrupted.

"When she informed me yesterday," John Woodley repeated with greater emphasis, "about your behaviour, I was disgusted. Disgusted!"

"She wasn't at work yesterday. She didn't tell you anything."

"Don't talk rubbish. Of course she was at work. You were the one who wasn't at work."

"She told me that she hadn't been at work yesterday. When I rang her up."

"Don't try to be clever. You know and I know what the situation is. Now, lay off Julie Grant or you'll be in big trouble."

"Get lost," said Graham.

The sand had vanished from the flat by the time he returned that evening. There was no trace of it anywhere. Not even under the bed.

Marc appeared. "Claudine's gone," he said.

"Where to?"

"She didn't say."

"Are you cut up about it?"

Marc seated himself in an armchair, the one Julie had occupied on her visits. He looked up at the ceiling. "I'll miss her," he said.

"Won't we all," said Graham.

Later that evening they smoked the rest of the hash and listened to music.

"Marc," said Graham, as blobs of intense colour drifted lazily in the air. "About Claudine."

"What about her?"

"Did she have any fetishes about salt? Or sand? Salt or sand?"

There was a long pause.

"What did you say?" asked Marc dreamily.

Graham couldn't remember. He giggled at his forgetfulness, and Marc joined in. They couldn't stop themselves.

They sat with their arms round each other. The music had come to an end, and the blobs of intense colour had drifted away.

"Are you gay?" asked Graham.

"I don't think so," said Marc drowsily. "I can't remember."

"I don't think you are. And I don't think I am. But if we aren't, why are

136

we sitting like this?"

"Because we're people," said Marc. "Sex doesn't come into it."

"Right," said Graham. "I see."

He sat and listened. The huge, green, amorphous thing had returned and was quietly humming to itself somewhere; Graham could not quite make out the tune, nor the direction it came from. Trying to listen to it was like watching something out of the corner of your eye.

Music again filled the room; Marc had put on some early Pink Floyd. Graham felt soft waves of sensation; he could not distinguish sights from sounds. Little dots of colour suddenly shot across his vision in brief double bursts. Reddish tinged with silver. It took him a while to realise that his landline was ringing.

He answered it.

"Graham? Graham?" Julie's voice sounded agitated. "Please help me, Graham."

Graham suppressed a desire to giggle. "What's happening?"

"Oh Graham, I'm really scared."

"There's nothing to be scared of. Everything is just..." He hunted for the right word. "Unscareful." He spoke with great deliberation. To speak was to wade through thick mud.

"Gavin's going to turn up," Julie said. Her voice was a little girl's whine. "I just know he is."

With an effort, Graham recalled who Gavin was.

"Gavin," he said, "is not a name to worry about. No one called Gavin could cause trouble. Now if his name was Mario or Dario, that's a different matter. You're sure he's not called Mario or Dario?"

"Please. I'm scared. What shall I do?"

"Hang on, I'll consult the oracle." Graham turned to Marc, but Marc had fallen asleep and could not be roused by a foot in the ribs.

"The oracle," said Graham sententiously down the phone, "is asleep. But don't worry, I know what to do. If you're worried about Mario – I mean Dario – popping up unexpectedly, you must ensure you're not in the place where he's liable to pop. Pop, pop, pop," he repeated vacuously. "Pop, pop, pop."

"What can I do, then? Where can I go?"

"Here," said Graham, ceasing to pop. "Come here. There's room enough for two."

"Could I?"

137

"Of course. I'll come and pick you up."

After a long search Graham located his car keys, but the difficulty he experienced in inserting the key into the ignition decided him against driving.

He walked to Julie's. She had packed an overnight bag, and they walked back to Graham's flat. In his right hand he carried her bag; his left arm was round her waist.

Marc was still asleep on the sitting room floor. They crept past him into the bedroom and went to bed. It was a tight squeeze in the single bed, which made matters more enjoyable. They had spoken very little.

viii

Graham drove Julie to work in the morning. She got out of the car a few hundred yards from the building in order to enter the place alone. They did not wish to be seen together. They had agreed that, should their paths cross during the working day, neither of them would do or say anything which might excite comment. When, on one occasion, they had to talk together on work matters, Graham took great delight in assuming a detached, impersonal air. His secret glee gave him superiority over the other members of staff.

At the end of the day, he left on his own. He emphasised the fact to Nick.

"Back to my bachelor pad," he said. "An evening on my tod. Just me and the telly. Dinner for one."

"Want to come back for a bite with me?" Nick offered. "If you're feeling lonely?"

"No, no thanks. Thanks all the same."

Down a side street at a prearranged spot, Julie awaited him. They drove to Whitmore Lane and briefly patrolled outside. Julie was afraid that Gavin might be waiting for her.

"He drives an old red Metro," she said.

"Not in evidence."

"I'll go in and get a few things, then."

"Need a hand?"

"No. You stay here. Just in case."

Twenty minutes later she re-emerged, staggering under the weight of two large suitcases. Graham went to assist.

"That it?" he said, heaving them onto the back seat of the car.

"Hang on, just a couple more things."

"Bloody hell."

The 'couple more things' turned out to be a couple of dozen more things. When the car was full, they drove back to Graham's. He cleared a space in his wardrobe and a couple of drawers for her clothes. They would not all go in.

Over a takeaway Indian, he studied Julie. She had been very ordinary at first, rather plain. Now she was pretty. And definitely older. Twenty-one, had she said? Twenty-two? Whichever, she was definitely nearer twenty-six or twenty-seven now – nearer his own age. Past the silly stage, but still dependent on him. He smiled.

"What are you grinning at?" she asked.

"Things," he mumbled.

She held up a forkful of food and playfully fed him. There was a shy look about her.

"I was right to trust you," she said. "I don't regret it."

"Of course."

"I feel safe."

"You are."

"Good."

The noise of Marc's harmonium could be heard. It did not wheeze and groan as much as formerly: he had corrected a number of faults.

Julie had not yet met Marc properly; Graham contemplated going to get him but decided against it. There would be time enough.

ix

The next day was Saturday. Someone had stolen Friday; it did not exist that week. When they woke up they made love, then Julie went out to shop, having cast aspersions on Graham's stock of convenience food. While she was out, Graham read the paper and puzzled over the chess problem.

The buzzer buzzed. Graham pressed the button. "Hello, yes?"

"It's me, Graham. Anne," came the tinny response through the intercom.

"Oh. Er, come up." Graham pressed the button to release the main door, then went to his own front door. Anne's arrival startled him; he had not been in contact with his former girlfriend since her marriage to the Italian waiter.

Mario or Dario or whatever the fellow's name was.

"What brings you here?" Graham asked as Anne pushed past him into the flat.

"I drove."

"I mean, what sequence of events? What chain of cause and effect? What concatenation of circumstances? What nexus of—"

"I got in the car," Anne spoke over him. "I started the engine. I put it into gear. I drove here."

"That explains it. You've grown. You never used to be that tall."

"Of course I haven't grown."

They were in the sitting room. Anne was taking off her coat, and now swirling her long hair about.

"I must have shrunk, then," said Graham. "What are you doing here?"

"I've left Henry."

"Who?"

"Henry. My husband."

"You mean Mario? Or is it Dario?"

Anne stared at him. "What are you on about? My husband is Henry, and I've left him."

"Oh. When was that?"

Anne looked at her watch. "Two hours thirty-eight minutes ago. I'd already packed a case. It's in the car. Go and bring it up for me."

"Are you staying here, then?"

"Of course I am."

Graham went down to her car. A beige suitcase was on the back seat, next to a massive drum of salt. It contained twenty-five kilos.

"No sand, though," said Graham as he carried the case upstairs.

Anne had gone through to the bedroom. "Whose are these?" she demanded, holding up items of Julie's underwear.

"Julie's."

"And who," Anne said, "is Julie?"

"She lives here."

"Oh, she does, does she? And what about me? Where am I supposed to sleep?"

"I hadn't thought of that," said Graham. "You'll have to sort it out with Julie."

"And where is she now, this tart of yours?"

140

"She's not a tart."

"I'll decide that."

Julie returned with the shopping. She looked cheerful, and had also bought herself a multicoloured woolly hat.

"Julie," said Graham. "Are you a tart?"

Julie stared at him. "That's not a nice thing to say. Of course not."

Graham turned to Anne. "There. I told you so."

But Anne and her suitcase had gone.

That evening, Julie said she would like to see Nick. Graham was in the middle of rolling a cigarette.

"Nick who?"

"You know. Nick. You work with him."

"What do you want to see him for?"

"I haven't seen him for a long time."

"You see him every day at work."

"Not socially."

"But you don't know him socially."

"Yes, I do. I told you – he's an old friend. I'll give him a ring."

After a brief phone call, Julie told Graham they would be meeting Nick at the Lamb and Flag. On their arrival they found Nick already at the bar, accompanied by Claudine.

"I didn't know you two knew each other," said Graham.

"Why shouldn't we?" said Nick.

"It seems highly suspicious," said Graham. "Perhaps it's a plant."

A round of drinks was bought.

"Someone covered my entire flat with salt the other day," said Graham. He looked round at the others to determine their reactions.

"I see the King of Sweden's been assassinated," said Nick.

"And sand," said Graham. Another look. They couldn't fool him.

"They've been beaming in from satellites," said Claudine, and burst into a Swedish love song. Two men with hats pulled down over their eyes started making notes in pocketbooks. Nick picked up a beer mat and tore a corner off it in a highly significant manner.

Claudine finished her Swedish love song.

"She's always asking me to go to bed with her," Graham complained.

"We must get married," said Julie. "You will marry me, won't you?"

"I see the King of Sweden's been assassinated again," said Nick.

"First salt, then sand," said Graham. "Just because I wouldn't go to bed with her."

Claudine launched into a Slavic dirge. Nick and Julie joined in. The two men with hats pulled down over their eyes slowly tapped their pocketbooks on the bar in time with the dirge.

"Won't anyone listen?" shouted Graham. He banged his glass down on the bar and went out into the street. A drizzling rain hadn't started to fall.

A short distance away, lights were glowing through the windows of a church hall. Graham found a meeting in progress. Three men on a dais at the front were directing operations; one was talking rapidly in a language Graham did not recognise, another translated into English, and a third interjected "Praise the Lord!" and "Hallelujah!" spasmodically. Other ejaculations arose from the main body of the hall, where two hundred or more people were kneeling, hands clasped together, eyes closed, faces raised. A number of people were leaving the congregation and going up to the front, there to kneel before the triumvirate.

Graham joined them.

The three elders now began to walk among the kneelers at the front, stopping at each one to place both hands on the head of the supplicant. One of the elders was John Woodley. He didn't look like John Woodley, but Graham knew for certain he *was* John Woodley. Graham looked up at him as he approached. There was no sign of recognition in John Woodley's eyes as he placed his hands on Graham's head and murmured something inaudible. Graham expected to feel a thrill of ecstasy, or at least a tiny shiver, but all he felt was his hair being ruffled. He got up and went to the back of the hall, where he sat on a tubular-metal chair with torn green canvas.

The John Woodley elder said a few words to the assembly. It was clearly a summary of a longer speech made at the beginning of the meeting.

"…for we do not know the hour of His coming!" he concluded.

This was Graham's moment. He leapt to his feet. "It's all right!" he called out loudly. "I'm here already, I've come."

There was a profound silence, then the John Woodley elder spoke again. "There will be an opportunity afterwards for all who have been up to the front, and any others who wish to, to talk individually with myself or one of the other brethren for spiritual guidance and counselling."

Graham sat down again.

"Meanwhile," continued the John Woodley elder, "we are going to sing number eighty-four in the blue book. Sorry, the yellow book."

They sang the hymn, in which they exhorted themselves to go forth and convert the vile heathen. Graham sang lustily. Vile heathens did not deserve to be converted, but he was feeling magnanimous.

Afterwards, one of the other elders approached him. "Perhaps you would care to talk things over?" he suggested.

"Certainly," said Graham. "What's troubling you?"

"I was wondering if anything was troubling *you*? Perhaps I can be of help?"

"There is the matter of the salt," Graham acknowledged.

"I see. The salt of the earth? We are indeed called upon to be the salt of the earth, and if the salt loses its flavour—"

"And sand," said Graham. "Salt and sand."

The elder looked thoughtful. "We are, of course, told by the prophets that the thoughts of God are more numerous than the sands. Perhaps that is what you are thinking of?"

"Salt and sand and bloody Swedish love songs," said Graham. "Just because I wouldn't."

"Could you explain a little further?"

"I came home and what do I find? The whole place streaming in salt. And that's the first time. Next time it's sand. Tons of the stuff. Salt and then sand. A plague. Two plagues."

"I think," said the elder slowly, "that you'd better see Brother Andrew. He is gifted with considerable insight and discernment."

He slipped away, soon to be replaced by the John Woodley elder who didn't look like John Woodley.

"Hullo, John," said Graham. "What are you doing in this set-up?"

"I am Brother Andrew. Now, how can I be of help?"

"I see. It's like a stage name, is it?"

"Brother Andrew is my name. I have no other."

"All right, suit yourself," said Graham. "So tell me, if you're so smart and discerning – why salt and sand? Did you put her up to it?"

"Perhaps you could tell me more about these…visions?"

"Not visions. The real thing. One day salt, your best rock crystal, sodium chloride in person, and the next day sand, or silicon dioxide if you like, which I don't. She wanted it, you see, and when I refused, this happens. Mind you, in her favour she has got bazookas the size of…well, bazookas. She must have roped Anne in on it somehow, but I haven't worked out how. Cunning, though,

I'll give her that."

John Woodley/Brother Andrew frowned.

"We must pray about it," he said. "We must seek guidance."

"You reckon? A spot of guidance?"

At the end of a long extempore prayer in which Graham was referred to several times as 'thy servant', John Woodley/Brother Andrew shook him by his hand. "I think it would be beneficial if you attended for regular spiritual guidance," he said. "And also, do come to our prayer meetings, when we can continue to offer this to the Lord."

He handed Graham a leaflet detailing the fellowship's various weekly meetings. There was some event or other on every night.

"Actually," said Graham, "I don't go in for a lot of prayer. Seeing as who I am, it's a bit too much like talking to myself."

x

Graham turned left. He did not turn right because the huge, green, amorphous thing was waiting for him in that direction. It had put on weight recently. He wandered around aimlessly until he came to a wooden bench outside a car park. On this bench he sat down and fell asleep.

When he awoke he was cold and stiff. His head ached, his mouth was dry. There was no sign of the huge, green, amorphous thing. It was early morning, and as he made his way back to his flat he passed two pedestrians.

"I see the King of Sweden's been assassinated," said one.

"So's Graham Ferrari," said the other.

It took him until ten o'clock to find his flat. Someone had moved it. Julie was not there. Graham curled up on his bed and fell asleep again, awaking in the late afternoon. After a bath, he walked round to Whitmore Lane.

"Oh, hello," said Julie.

"Can I come in?" said Graham.

She hesitated and glanced behind her. Graham got the impression that she was not alone.

"Well…" she said.

Graham barged past her and discovered that his impression had been doubly correct: there were two other people present. One was a shadowy male whose features Graham could not quite discern – he always seemed to be out of

144

Graham's direct line of vision. The other person present was Anne.

"What are you doing here?" he asked her.

"I came," said Anne. She was sitting on Julie's bed.

"We've been talking about you," said Julie.

"What about me?" asked Graham.

"What about you?" said the two women in unison. They laughed. Graham didn't.

"Who's that?" he asked, trying to indicate the shadowy male.

The two women answered simultaneously. "It's Gavin. We're getting married tomorrow," said Julie. "It's Henry. We were married last October," said Anne.

The shadowy Gavin/Henry male would still not come into Graham's line of vision, and Graham could not turn his head to look directly at him. Gavin/Henry did not speak.

"What happened after I left the pub last night?" asked Graham.

"Nothing happened," said Anne.

"You weren't there," Graham told her.

"Nothing," confirmed Julie.

"Why did you come back here?" Graham said. "Why didn't you come back to my place?"

"Henry was here," said Anne. "That's why. Where else would you expect me to be?"

"Ah," said Graham sagaciously. It was clearly a case of pawn to queen four.

"I think it's time to go," said Anne. "Come on, Henry."

"And take the knight on bishop three with you while you're about it," said Graham.

Anne left. The shadowy male left with her and also remained behind.

"You must go as well," Julie said to Graham.

Graham went up to her and put his arm round her, then guided her to the bed. She did not resist. They started kissing. She clung to him tighter and tighter, and the sequence of events was as before.

xi

The doorbell rang, accompanied by several heavy blows. A voice shouted. Graham awoke, groaning; he was alone in his own bed. He swung himself out of it and went to answer the door, wondering who had buzzed whoever it was into the flats. Two policemen stood outside. They ascertained that his name was Graham Ferrari and asked if he would accompany them to the station to help with their enquiries.

"Can I see your ID?" said Graham.

The two policemen produced official-looking cards. One of the policemen was Nick, the other was Marc.

"I didn't recognise you," said Graham.

A third policeman arrived. It was the shadowy male, Gavin/Henry, and he handed over a birth certificate. It was blank. Graham handed all the documents back.

"You know a Miss Julie Grant?" said policeman Nick.

"I've met her once or twice," said Graham.

"Earlier this morning she was the victim of an assault of a sexual nature."

"I'm sorry to hear it," said Graham.

"And we believe that you can help us with our investigation."

"I doubt it," said Graham. "I'm not actually a policeman."

"You were the last person to see her before the assault occurred."

"When was it?" said Graham.

"Come on," said Policeman Marc. "Get your clothes on. We're going down to the station."

"Euston or St Pancras?"

Gavin/Henry had remained silent, always on the periphery, but Graham knew he was in charge. As Graham dressed, strains of a Swedish love song were audible from below.

"Tell her to shut up," said Graham. But the singing had already stopped and Claudine herself was present.

"I thought you'd gone," said Graham.

"He wouldn't go to bed with me," she said accusingly. Policeman Marc wrote it down in his notebook.

"Why wouldn't you go to bed with this lady?" he asked.

"She didn't say please," said Graham.

"She didn't say please," repeated the policeman, noting it down.

"And bloody Slavic dirges!" shouted Graham.

"And bloody Slavic dirges," repeated the policeman, noting it down.

They went to the police station, where he was asked for his full name.

"Brother Andrew," he replied.

"I must caution you," said Policeman Nick, "that anything you say will be taken down in writing and ignored. I want a full account of all your activities: where you've been, who you've seen, what you've done."

"Starting from when I was born…" began Graham.

"From five o'clock yesterday afternoon up until now," Policeman Marc said.

"Well, the last half hour's easy. I've been with you lot."

"We're more interested in what you were up to between, let's say, six o'clock and eight o'clock last evening."

"I don't remember."

"You'll have to remember."

"Ask Julie."

"She's named you as her attacker."

Innumerable questions followed. Graham did not understand them.

"Want a smoke?" Policeman Marc said. "I've enough for a good one." He had pudgy fingers but rolled a beautiful joint. Graham recalled some of Marc's plaintive songs and began to weep.

"Too late to be sorry," snapped Policeman Nick.

A policewoman entered bearing a tray. It was Julie. In uniform. She didn't look like Julie, but Graham recognised her thighs.

"Please help me, Graham," she said, "I haven't anyone to turn to. John Woodley keeps fondling me. I like you fondling me."

Graham reached out his hands to oblige. Someone shouted and the two policemen leapt on him. They seemed to enjoy restraining him. The knee of one of them slipped and Graham's leg went numb.

"Don't leave any visible marks," he heard the other policeman say. "Remember your training."

"Why don't you like Swedish love songs?" demanded the interrogator. "Are you racist?"

"Certainly not," said Graham. "I'm Capricorn. Which is all balls." He stood up. "I think I'll be on my way now. Goodbye."

There was a short struggle. Graham's head banged against the corner of the desk.

xii

He was in a small, quiet room when he awoke. He was lying on a bed, with two or three blankets covering him. A round clock on the wall ticked. Graham's own clothes had been taken away, and a constable in attendance handed him some others. As he dressed, the constable left the room, and presently a middle-aged man entered. He wore a charcoal-coloured suit and carried a briefcase, from which he drew out a folder containing several sheets of paper. The constable returned and stood by the door.

The man in the charcoal suit introduced himself as Dr Speller before he metamorphosed into Nick, then into Marc, then Gavin/Henry. Each time Graham looked at him, he was someone different. Graham watched him while pretending not to, intent on catching him at the moment of change. But Dr Speller was cunning. He waited each time for Graham to be distracted by something – a noise outside the room, the light flickering, a patch of moss growing on the wall – then he changed. Instantaneously.

He started to ask Graham a series of questions at the wrong speed, often in a foreign language in order to catch him out. But Graham was himself too cunning and replied in a different foreign language. Check.

The policewoman came in. It was Anne.

"I'm going back to Henry," she said.

"Henry?"

"I said, are you hungry?"

"Hungry?"

"I'm Mrs Anne Waugh now, remember?"

"I forgot."

"Well, are you feeling Henry?"

"I'm not gay."

"This is important to you, is it?" interposed Dr Speller. "You're afraid of being thought homosexual? How long have you had these fears of being thought homosexual?"

Graham did not answer.

"How close are you to your male friends?" Dr Speller persisted.

Graham recalled sitting with his arm round Marc and Marc's arm round him.

"About half an inch," he said. "It's because we're people. Sex doesn't come into it."

"Now, Mr Ferrari." Dr Speller started on a new tack.

"I'm Will Zakir," said Graham. "I play chess with Graham Ferrari. Do you play chess?"

"No," said Anne, now Julie. "I used to know the moves, though."

The room had become crowded with people: Marc, Nick, John Woodley, Claudine, the King of Sweden, Anne, two men with hats pulled down over their eyes, a decomposing writer of Swedish love songs.

Will Zakir stepped forward. "Back to the bunsens!" he announced.

The clock ticked on. A bishop slid out diagonally, chased by three or four pawns which looked like three or four pawns. Everyone was talking at once. Voices rose in competition with each other. Mouths moving, features shifting. A babble of words, of sounds criss-crossing the room. He could see them criss-crossing, fine wires, vibrating like guitar strings, releasing sounds with every vibration until the room was packed to capacity with the fine wires, with sound, with people. They swirled about him.

Graham stood up. "I don't think I want this," he said.

No one heard him. No one responded. The babble intensified. Nick and Marc and Julie and Anne and the King of Sweden and Claudine and Dr Speller and people and people and people were shouting, arguing, demanding. There was a wailing sound, then a chant, and everywhere he looked they were facing him, chanting, swaying backwards and forwards and chanting. He was hemmed in, trapped, at their mercy.

"I don't want this!" he repeated loudly.

Louder and louder their voices. More insistent their tones. Faces distorted, hands outstretched.

There was only one course of action open to him. The one, final, desperate course of action. The only way, and they hadn't realised. None of them had realised.

All he had to do was dispense with his name. With all names. Without a name he would be unreachable. He would be without a handle, and couldn't be held. Not by anyone. He would be free.

In that instant, he renounced his name. Discarded it, sloughed it off, stepped away from it. He was no longer Graham Ferrari, he was ————

The babble ceased abruptly. The room had emptied. No noise, no fine wires, no people, no clock. Nothing.

But outside, and inside, and all around, the huge, green, amorphous thing lurked and bided its time.

Scripts

Drinks Break

(Jack is sitting with a drink to hand. Johnnie enters, also with a drink. He sits.)

Jack
Johnnie? *Johnnie Walker?*

Johnnie
Jack Daniels! Well, well. Good to see you, *Madeira* old thing! How's life?

Jack
Not very *rosé*, I'm afraid.

Johnnie
You do look rather down in *vermouth*. What *ales* you?

Jack
It's *bloody Mary*. She's only gone and left me.

Johnnie
She 'asn't!

Jack
Shiraz!

Johnnie

Your marriage is *on the rocks*? What happened?

Jack

She ran off with a *Bénédictine*.

Johnnie

Great *scotch*! Which one?

Jack

Dom Pérignon.

Johnnie

Is he the one who got a *Blue Nun* into trouble?

Jack

Yeah. And what's more, they've absconded in my car.

Johnnie

Vodka? That's a bit *Chablis.*

Jack

It makes me want to *Spumante*. But I told her straight – if you go, I'm not going to shed a single *Tia, Maria.*

Johnnie

Absolut! That's the *spirit!* But obviously you're still *bitter*? I would *advocaat* Sauterne.

Jack

Sauterne?

Johnnie

Sauterne the other cheek.

Jack

Nah! When I think about it I get angrier and *sangria.* I've a good

mind to get myself a *shotgun*. Or possibly a good
strong bow.

Johnnie
Tequila?

Jack
No, just to frighten her.

Johnnie
That's a bit *whisky*.

Jack
I want to wipe the *Smirnoff* her face... Ach, *Pernod*
attention, I'm just not feeling very *cordial*. What's this music they're
playing?

Johnnie
Bach's *Limoncello* concerto.

Jack
So it is... But how about you? Are you still seeing the
lovely Gina?

Johnnie
Gina Tonic?

Jack
Yeah – I always thought she was a bit of a *hot toddy*.

Johnnie
Ah, well, she moved to *Manhattan* to be with *Jim Beam*.

Jack
Oh, the pole vaulter? Ah, yeah...what was his nickname?

Johnnie

High balls.

Jack

You heard about his accident? Bit of a *rum* do...

Johnnie

...part way through a jump his pole *Schnapps*...

Jack

...and he lands right on a *Bishop's Finger*! And now he's no longer able to *Buck's Fizz*. At least, I think that's what his mother said. So he's definitely sadder...

Johnnie

Budweiser... And poor old Gina. Such a *sparkling* lass.

Jack

Au *Cointreau*, she was never much of a *mixer*. Anyway, look, I'd better *Moselle* along. I must get to the dentist to collect *aperitif*.

Johnnie

I ought to get *bock* as well. I'm *absinthe* without leave. Santé!

Jack

Bottoms up!

Dead Safe

(Enter a dark-suited male of indeterminate age and gloomy aspect. He is carrying a clipboard, to which are attached several sheets of regulations that he consults. He addresses the audience.)

Are you all here? Good. Well, it is my duty, albeit not necessarily my pleasure, to welcome each and every one of you to the Afterlife. *Stop snivelling at the back!*

You are probably wondering why, since you are dead, you are gathered here in this fashion, rather than continuing on your various journeys up…or down…or round and round – depending upon your belief system, or lack of belief system, during your recent period of earthly embodiment. What you believed then does indeed affect what happens to you now.

I said *stop snivelling at the back*!

The reason you are here in this antechamber, as it were, is quite simple: I have recently been appointed as the 'Health and Safety Officer for the Afterlife', and it is my task to ensure that your stay in eternity will be both safe and healthy. I will admit straight away that when I first learned of this appointment, I was somewhat sceptical: the concept of 'health and safety' still seems to me, quite frankly, to run counter to the original purpose of the destination for which the vast majority of you here are heading.

Oh, *do stop snivelling*, Professor Dawkins! None of us is impressed by your Victor Meldrew impersonation! '*I don't believe it!*' Look around you. Study the empirical evidence…

As I was saying, quite how anyone can be considered both safe and healthy while sloshing around upside down in a vat of boiling brimstone does somewhat escape me, but apparently the whole point of this health and safety malarkey is to put a stop to such innocent fun. Outmoded, apparently. No longer 'relevant'. Insufficiently inclusive.

I used to be 'Supreme Ruler' of the infernal regions, I'll have you know, with more minions than the Civil Service to carry out my every order, but following strong representations over the past couple of centuries to the Almighty from a bunch of wishy-washy, do-gooding, social-working, person-centred, hermeneutically obsessed, form-critical, radical liberal pinko woke theologians, what were the infernal regions have been redesignated the mildly uncomfortable, slap-on-the-wrist-provided-it-doesn't-leave-a-visible-mark regions. Moreover, I have been ludicrously failed on several 'key competencies' deemed necessary for my job description, such as 'empathy' and 'non-judgementalism'.

Empathy and non-judgementalism in the infernal regions? Excuse me, but am I missing something? Apparently complaints have been made about me by a number of service users...oh yes, 'service users'. It has been deemed politically incorrect to refer to everyone who has died as, collectively, 'the dead'. So you will, no doubt, be delighted to learn that although you *have* died, you are no longer simply 'the dead' – instead, you have been redesignated as 'Afterlife Service Users'.

Well, it happens that a number of miserable snowflake 'Afterlife Service Users' have reported on their 'Satisfaction Feedback Forms' that I have an 'attitude problem'. No. I do *not* have an 'attitude problem'. I have an attitude. *They* have the problem.

Anyway, be that as it may, I'd better get a move on, I haven't got all day...well, actually, come to think of it I *have* got all day, I've got eternity...

So: health and safety in the Afterlife. Here we go. As you proceed on your way, I must draw your attention to a number of hazards. First, the river Lethe. Don't go drinking the waters of the river Lethe. I forget exactly why, but I know it does constitute a hazard.

When crossing the river Styx with Sharon the boatperson, *After*life-jackets must be worn. And do not attempt to extinguish the river Phlegethon. It's a river of fire – that's what it's *meant* to do. Which reminds me: the Afterlife has been designated a no-smoking zone. Any smokers among you will have to wait to be reincarnated – if that's your belief system. If it *isn't* your belief system, tough.

Now, specifically for those of you heading upwards to the empyrean realms, full of joy and happiness, allegedly – not that any of you lot are going to make it, as far as I can see, but I still have to give you the spiel. First: wings. If you are allergic to feathers, please inform the angelic host, who will issue you with non-allergenic alternatives – no doubt made from knitted Quorn or tofu.

Halos. Halos are to be worn at all times – *above* the head. Nowhere else. That is how they are designed. They are not to be used as a species of celestial Frisbee.

Harps. You will be issued with a harp, and a harp has multiple nylon and steel strings held under considerable tension. These are not to be used either for slicing cheese or garotting unmusical neighbours. Beware of excessive harp playing: although you are encouraged to make a joyful noise unto the Lord, research has indicated that joyful noises 24/7 result in tinnitus, insomnia and profound depression. So a twenty-minute break once every seven days is now obligatory.

Golden crowns: the casting down of golden crowns around a glassy sea has now been discontinued – they constitute a tripping hazard.

As for those of you heading downwards – that's virtually everyone here, I reckon – you are advised to avoid the worm that never dies: it can give you a nasty nip. And under no circumstances must you climb over the safety barrier that has now been erected around the bottomless pit... I ask you, what's the point of a bottomless pit if a safety barrier is put round it to stop Afterlife Service Users being cast into it? It completely negates its purpose. There's even talk of the bottomless pit being fitted with a false bottom. Excuse me? Doesn't a bottomless pit with *any* sort of bottom constitute a logical paradox? A contradiction in terms? Whatever. I am contractually obliged to draw it to your attention.

For those of you who are going neither up nor down but around and around on the endless cycle of death and rebirth, you will be delighted to hear that facilities have now been installed for the overhauling and servicing of your endless cycle. It's called the 'endless cycle repair shop'. Electric endless cycles are also available. Please ensure your endless cycle is regularly inspected and serviced by the relevant authorities and that you are issued with a certificate permitting you to ride it during your times of non-embodiment. I assure you that these procedures will result in your post-death experience being a lot...*karma*. Just my little joke...

In conclusion, I must ask that before any of you continue your journey up, down or endlessly around, you sign the contractual agreement that should anything untoward befall you during eternity, you will not pursue legal redress at the court of heaven.

Before you continue on your way, it is now my duty to wish you all a safe and healthy Afterlife throughout eternity…

But I'm bloody well not going to.

Author! Author!

(Enter a presenter, who sits on a chair, opens a book, and addresses the audience.)

Have you ever been embarrassed at social gatherings when the talk turns to literature and you've not heard of the authors being discussed? If so, then this introductory course of significant authors is for you. Simply commit the following short story to memory, and the names of over seventy giants of literature will be at your command.

So, to start with the obvious ones, please stop *Tolkien*, and no more *Larkin* about…

One bright *Somerset Maugham*, after playing *Tennyson* the lawn, *Lewis* and *Carroll* set off for a *Nietzsche* ramble across a *Fielding* and into a dark *Forrester*. But they had not gone far when the weather suddenly *Turgenev Grimm*. The *Wyndham* blew *Wilder*, *C.P. Snow* fell on them, and *Sassoon* they had lost their *Hemingway*.

"*Arnold Bennett!*" exclaimed Lewis. "This *Shaw* makes things *Confucius*. We must go *Thurber* on."

But suddenly Carroll sneezed: "*Isherwood! Ishiguro!! John Grisham!!!*" and she looked quite *Haggard*. So she lay down on a patch of *Graham Greene Günter Grass* by a babbling *Rupert Brooke* and had a quick *Rudyard Kipling*… just so. When she awoke, she realised that all was not *H.G. Wells*, because Lewis was looking *Sterne*.

"I've decided to *Donleavy* you," he said, speaking more in *Thoreau* than in *Salinger*.

Now, *she* didn't want to listen, but *E… M… Forster!*

"It's not your *Faulkner*," he continued. "It's mine. For years I've re*Proust* my true *Will Self*, not knowing whether I was *Cummings* or *Golding*."

"*Stoppard*!" she cried. "Have you lost your *Whit, man*? Are you my friend or *Defoe*? All this talk, but what are your *Wordsworth*? You're making a *Montaigne* out of a *Molière*."

"I have no *Joyce*," said Lewis. "You no longer drive me *Wilde*. I thought you would, but how can a *Mantel*?"

"You *Rattigan*! You *Stan Barstow*!" she *Hermann Hessed*. "Must you *Brecht* my heart? Your *Longfellow* used to make my *Fanny Burney*, but now you have the *Galsworthy* to say I am a *Blyton* your life. I hate you through and *Theroux*. This means *Waugh*."

"Don't let's have a *J. K. Rowling*," said Lewis. "I already *Rousseau* much."

"*Orwell*," said Carroll, "you must paddle your own *Camus*."

So *Sayers*, she continued on her *Owen* and caught the *Twain Homer*. She now lives in *Marlowe* working in an Italian restaurant – she always had quite a *Pasternak*. Lewis has married a *Saki Trollope* who's quite a *Marvell*, though he really prefers a spot of *Updike*.

That is the end of today's *Lessing*, so good *Byron* for now, and see you *Du Maurier*.

Saints and Theologians

(Enter a sports commentator.)

Hello and welcome to what promises to be an exciting afternoon of racing here at Aintree, and you join us with just a few minutes to go before the start of the Saints' and Theologians' Crown of Glory Steeplechase. We do have a field of extremely distinguished runners for you, all competing for the right to wear a Crown of Glory for the next twelve months of eternity. And now here they come, being led out from their stalls by their guardian angels.

Straight away I can see Dame Julian of Norwich. What a revelation she's been recently – and a lovely little mover as well. She's followed by St Swithin, who by all accounts is very much under the weather – and will continue to be so for the next forty days and forty nights. St Ignatius is still doing his exercises, but St Vitus comes dancing out in his inimitable way, and next is St Pancras – a surprise entrant today because in this sort of company St Pancras is competing somewhat above his station. I can see the Wesley brothers, John and Charles: some commentators believe they are completely bonkers, but I'm not so sure – I think there's Methodist in their madness. They're followed out by the mediaeval scholar and theologian Peter Abelard, with his pretty little filly, Heloise. He claims that Heloise is simply his pupil, but he has been going to confession an awful lot since meeting her. And now a great roar goes up for the crowd's favourite – it's England's patron saint, dressed in women's clothing: St George with drag on. And with him is the former Archbishop of Cape Town, Desmond – looking very fetching in his tutu.

Now, if you want to have a wager with the on-course bookie, honest Blaise

Pascal, the question is: who do you put your cassock on? John Calvin, of course, is determined to win. Indeed, he claims that the result is a foregone conclusion, believing himself to be a dead certainty – well, he's certainly dead, but clearly expecting to make a comeback. St Thomas is doubtful, the Venerable Bede is surely somewhat too venerable, and St Bernard has gone to the dogs. But don't dismiss Martin Luther – he's quite a reformed character. But if you take my advice, you'll put your hair shirt on St Paul, following his recent performance on the Damascus Road when he ran an absolute blinder.

Well, they're under starter's orders...and they're off! St Francis of Assisi takes an early lead, followed by Thomas Aquinas, Meister Eckhart, St Augustine and the Wesley brothers, but Hildegard of Bingen is coming up on the inside, and as they round their first catechism, St Francis is pulling away from Aquinas and Eckhart. St Augustine is maintaining his original doctrine of sin – but something has happened to St Francis! St Francis is definitely in trouble! He has come to a complete halt... I think he must have shed a sandal – no, no! It's not that! St Francis has simply stopped to feed the birds! Very self-sacrificing, because it's somewhat scuppered his chances and he'll really need a miracle now as the rest of the field streams past him... They're now approaching their first leap of faith...and over they go: Aquinas, Augustine, Eckhart, Hildegard, Wesley, Wesley, and now Matthew, Mark, Luke and John are getting in on the Acts...but ah! Here comes a challenge from Peter Abelard! Abelard is making tremendous theological strides as he overtakes the four evangelists, overtakes John Wesley, overtakes Charles Wesley, and now he's gaining on Hildegard of Bingen...but Hildegard hikes up her habit and puts on a very impressive turn of speed! I don't know what they put in their breakfast porridge in these mediaeval convents, but it's given her more than a touch of the Soul's Awakening. But Abelard is still gaining on her as they all now have to clear the notorious 'temptations of the flesh'! Thomas Aquinas is still in the lead and he safely clears the temptations! Here comes Augustine right behind him – and Augustine has stumbled! Augustine nearly comes a cropper because of the temptations of the flesh, but he's recovered himself well and he clears the temptations at the second attempt – which means that under the regulations he's still being... chaste. Hildegard of Bingen and Meister Eckhart clear the temptations easily enough, but here comes Peter Abelard...it's going to be a challenge for him... oh, and he's fallen! Peter Abelard has fallen at the temptations of the flesh! He's fallen for Heloise! ... In fact, he's fallen on Heloise! No surprise there, I must say – so Abelard and Heloise are out of the running...and into the bushes...and here come the seraphim with buckets of cold water.

As the remaining runners pass through an unusually thick cloud of unknowing and enter a long dark night of the soul, I can see that John Bunyan is starting to make progress and Teilhard de Chardin is proving quite a phenomenon…but what's happening now? What is happening out there on the track? It's an angel! An angel has manifested itself in the middle of the track, an angel wielding a flaming sword! None of the runners can get past, and there's a tremendous theological pile-up! Dogma flying all over the place! Schisms left, right and centre! This is quite simply a divine shambles, but if you'll bear with me an announcement is being made…and there has just been a revelation that the race shall not be to the swift, but somewhat controversially the last shall be first! Bit unexpected, that – not very orthodox, and there are bound to be protestations. Let's hope they can sort it out before Judgement Day or there'll be hell to pay.

However, while we wait for confirmation, I'm going to hand you back to the Archangel Gabriel at the Paradise Studios. So farewell, and Godspeed!

The Final Supervision

(The university room of PhD supervisor Dr Schadenfreude. Enter his supervisee, Robert Spiggot.)

Schadenfreude

Ah, Robert, come in. Good to see you again. It's been...quite some time since we last met.

Spiggot

Hello, Prof! Yes, I'm sorry I had to cancel the last two or three supervisions...

Schadenfreude

...or four or five. This is actually the first one you've managed to get to in two years.

Spiggot

Things have been a bit tricky at home. What with Mummy, you know. But here I am at last.

Schadenfreude

At, indeed, last. Take a seat, Robert, take a seat. Yes, you may sit on it... That's right, well done. Now, I asked you to come along today because I see from my records that you've been pursuing your doctorate for almost three years, but I have yet to see anything on your chosen topic of, er...of, er...

Spiggot

'The Influence of the Nicene Creed on the Silent Movies of Buster Keaton: A Pre-Post-Modern Symbiotic Approach.'

Schadenfreude

Yeees. Fascinating. Now, have you got anything to show me *this* time on such an interesting, not to say utterly meaningless, topic?

Spiggot

Not as such. (*He taps his head.*) I've got it all up here, though!

Schadenfreude

But nothing down here, where it counts, on the page? Manifest in the inter-subjective world, as one might say?

Spiggot

Not in so many words.

Schadenfreude

Not in *any* words, apparently. The trouble is, Robert, you are rapidly approaching the deadline – and I use the term advisedly – by when your thesis has to be submitted; and if, or rather *when*, you are failed, not only would that be a blow to you, but it would also reflect extremely badly on the department. We would get what is technically known as 'a black mark'.

Spiggot

Oh dear. Mummy wouldn't be happy for me to be responsible for a black mark. Is there anything I can do about it, Prof?

Schadenfreude

Since you mention it, yes, there is! You will be aware of the biblical precept that it is better for one man to die than for an entire university department to receive a black mark?

Spiggot

Er...is it?

Schadenfreude

Thus saith the Lord – or 'vice chancellor', as we call her. But the splendid news is that you have been unanimously selected by everyone in the department to *be* that one man.

Spiggot

Gosh, have I? Mummy will be pleased.

Schadenfreude

It's a win-win situation. You will receive your doctorate...

Spiggot

I will?

Schadenfreude

Of the post-obit variety, naturally. Posthumous, that is to say. But *summa cum laude*, of course...and the department will *not* in consequence receive a black mark, but instead a sympathy vote at the next interdepartmental carve-up of rapidly dwindling resources. And as a bonus, Mummy will be pleased – *your* mummy, that is; mine couldn't give a flying fart. And think of the advantages of a post-obit degree: no endless redrafting of your thesis, no lying awake in bed at three in the morning overcome with the utter ghastly futility of it all, no viva with impenetrably impertinent questions from some upstart external examiner eager to score debating points...

Spiggot

I'd never thought of it like that before.

Schadenfreude

Oh I have. Many times. Many, many times...

Spiggot

I think it's all terribly decent of you, Prof. But what is the exact procedure? Do I have to submit another proposal?

Schadenfreude

Good God, no! Nothing like that, *please*. No, it's all very straightforward: I carelessly leave a pearl-handled revolver, fully loaded, in this unlocked, open drawer of my desk while I go down the corridor to make us some coffee, and while I am gone...well, I don't need to spell it out, do I?

Spiggot

Yes, you do need to spell it out.

Schadenfreude

Ah, I was forgetting – you obtained your first degree with loyalty points from Sainsbury's, didn't you?

Spiggot

No, I did not! Mummy shops at Waitrose.

Schadenfreude

Indeed. Nevertheless, to spell it out: you spot the revolver in the open drawer when I'm not in the room, you take it out to examine it more closely, being a keen student of all things military...

Spiggot

But I'm not.

Schadenfreude

You are now...and just as you are peering down the barrel, it regrettably goes off.

Spiggot

Bang!

Schadenfreude

Making a sound similar to that which you have just uttered. Result? Incontrovertible evidence that, contrary to widespread belief in the department, you did have brains, albeit now all over my whiteboard, and a few weeks later, at the graduation ceremony, it's Robert Spiggot PhD.

Spiggot
That's wonderful, Prof. And so straightforward.

Schadenfreude
That's settled then: coffee, open drawer, gun, bang! PhD for you,
extra funding for us. Now, as there won't be the need for any more
supervisions, I'll congratulate you now on your highly successful but
tragically brief academic career, and bid you, I trust literally, *adieu*.
I'll just go and make that coffee, then.

Spiggot
Right ho, Prof. No sugar for me.

Schadenfreude
How very true.

Oxymoronic

(Enter the company chairman, Dr Ernest Flippant. He addresses the audience.)

Ladies, gentlemen, here at Oxymorons *Unlimited Ltd,* the *definite uncertainty* in the *present future* of our *firm's soft*ware requires us all to be *fearfully brave* and *desperately cautious.* Our *unprincipled principal* rivals are growing *stronger weekly,* while our *positively negative* attitude has led to an *upswing* in the *downgrading* of *understaffed overseers* and, *even odder,* a *speed-up* in the *slowdown* of *closing openings.* This *strangely normal standing situation facing us behind our backs* is caused by the *tight slackers* who have been leaving *early lately,* thus making the *pretty ugly divisions multiply* with each *succeeding failure.*

Now then, I have the *lowdown* from a *high-up* who should be *along shortly,* but he's at *present absent* having caught his *ear there* in a *dangerous safe.* He considers our *overheads underhand* and *fairly foul, stupidity-wise,* and his *unbelievably credible* yet *distinctly muffled additional deduction* is that we have too many *castles in the air that never get off the ground.*

I was taken by this *affront aback,* and although the *singular multiplicity* of *questionable answers* and *concrete solutions* is, to put it *baldly, hair-raising,* we must not take this *gigantic slight lying down, notwithstanding* the *clearly murky outlook inside.* We must keep our *appeaser accused* by each playing *a part together,* for the *greatly belittled truth lies* in *virgin* fields *pregnant* with possibilities. Good night and *good grief!*

Group Work

(Enter a male personal growth group facilitator carrying a cushion. He addresses the audience as his group.)

You have all brought your beanbags with you, haven't you? Cushions or pillows to sit on. It's important that we all sit on our cushions together, on the floor, because it symbolises that as human beings we are all on the same level. *(He places his cushion on a stool and sits on it.)*

Welcome, everyone, to the Self-Awareness and Personal Growth Encounter Group with Transpersonal Psychodynamic New Age Crystals. For beginners. My name is *Richard*, but you can call me...*Dick*! And I am the group 'facilitator'. Now, don't be frightened by that term. All it means is that as a facilitator I am here simply to...facilitate...those things that need... facilitating by a...facilitator.

Okay, it's time for us to move on to our group bonding, and for that we are going to...*you* are going to...do a trust exercise. I think you'll find the door is locked. And so are the windows. So if you will just rejoin the group? Thank you. We do seem to have a major problem with trust, don't we? So we'll start with some group sharing.

I'll begin by saying how affirmed I feel that I have given myself permission to risk interrelating with all of you, and I look forward to some authentic self-actualisation by dialoguing with my inner child. According to the stars I'm a Cancer; according to the Chinese New Year I'm a Rat; and according to the Myers-Briggs personality typology based on Jung, I'm an S.H.I.T.

Well, that's me in a nutshell. Who would like to share next? Yes? And you

175

are? Juliet! Welcome, Juliet. What a lovely name you have. And what is it that you bring to the group, Juliet? Uh-huh…uh-huh…yeah? So, you're into feng shui…the Tarot…and organic car maintenance. Uh-huh. And you're currently in a central dyadic relationship. Right. Is your significant other here? He's not? And that's because? Because he's an insensitive jerk who couldn't get in touch with his real self…even if he had one. Which you very much doubt? Uh-huh. Juliet, I must be congruent with my inner processes and share with you that not all men are insensitive jerks, and that…that…that's a very attractive little leather number you're wearing, I must say…and that some men can be very caring and sensitive and warm…very warm. Very, very warm. Um, thank you for sharing that with us, Juliet.

Who would like to share next? Yes? And you are? Pete! Hi, Pete! Tell us about yourself… You're into macrobiotic bungee jumping? Just the once. And what do you want to share with the group about your psyche? Ah, no, Pete, no. We don't use the word 'problems', do we, group? No, we don't! We reconstrue them as latent self-actualisation potentialities. Think of them as friends to guide us along life's…rich…tapestry. Tell us about your *friends*, Pete. Uh-huh…uh-huh…yeah?…uh-huh…with a *camel*?!…uh-huh… Well, Pete, you really have got a basinful of prob…a wide range of friends, haven't you? But, you know, it's time you started to own them, isn't it? Oh yes it is. Pete, I think you're in denial…oh yes you are.

Yes, thank you, Pete… I said *thank* you… So who's sharing next? And you are? Billy! What are you sharing with us, Billy? I hear you Billy, I really hear you… Did anyone else hear Billy? Billy has just said that he thinks that I am a complete pillock. Well, Billy, I'm going to reflect that back to you: *I* think *you're* a complete pillock… Could someone lend Billy a tissue, please? Now, Billy, when I said that you're a complete pillock, you burst into tears. That tells me that there is something in your karma that needs resolving, and the group is here to allow your psyche to find its authentic voice. To do this, we need to surf the existential plane of reality, so close your eyes, Billy, breathe deeply to tune in to the energies of the universe, and allow yourself to become aware of the first time someone called you a complete pillock… When was that, Billy? When did someone first call you a complete pillock? Uh-huh? At the *last* personal growth group you attended? Well, Billy, why do you think people are always calling you a complete pillock? That's right! It's because you *are* a complete pillock. That is a truly meaningful breakthrough in your self-understanding, Billy, and I'm sure the group can resonate with it. Can't you, group? Oh yes you can!

Okay, group, that's enough for now. We're going to take a break to stretch our auras, retune our mantras and reconnect with our inner gods and goddesses, then in the next session you'll be doing some primal screaming as I get in touch with your inner wallets. Rock on.

Due to Ronomy

(A clergyman addresses the congregation.)

Good *evensong*, and once again it's me, *Harry Lujah*, so *parson* the good news. *Te Deum*'s sermon is on driving, but first you must *a choir* a car. I suggest you in*vestry* in a Ford *Anglican* or a *Mini-ster*. You must *disciple* which. *Psalm* families have two cars – one is for *hymn*, and the other is *hearse*.

Always obey road *sins*, e.g. no *rite* turn, no *lectern*, and always halt at major *rood* ahead. Now, if you are out driving in the country and feel like a quick *epistle* in the *bushel* – a *wee free* – don't under any *circumcisions* park on a grass *verger*, by a Belisha *deacon*, or on a hump-backed *bishop*. It's a *cardinal* sin, so please *refrain*. All these *commandments* are in the Highway *Creed*, issued by the *Monastery* of Transport.

Vicar will be *Jew* for a *service* when it's *dean pastor* thousand miles, otherwise it *stalls* and the engine will *diocese* up, or *verse*. If by *chancel* this happens, there are *abbot* five or *sexton* ways to *rectory* the *treble*, but my *Methodist* is second to *nun*. Top up the *aisle*, wipe away the *surplice*, and that should *curate*. So get *dean* to work with *a nude vicar*…I mean, renewed vigour. *Pew!*

Also, check the *spire* tyre and *altar* the speedo-*mitre*, being very *Gentile*. But don't *temple* with the *rev* counter. *Passover* to a mechanic, but the *Pentecost* will be *steeple*.

Well, that's all. It's been *Magnificat* talking to you. I've *holy* enjoyed it, so *rabbi*! And now for a *mass exodus*!

Amazing!

(Enter a popular TV scientist.)

Hello, and welcome to another amazing episode in our groundbreaking series, *The Amazing World of Science*! And today we are looking at the amazing cutting-edge advances taking place by the merging of two established and highly respected disciplines: quantum physics and culinary science. This amazing, revolutionary new discipline goes by the name of 'quantum cookery'.

The seminal text for this discipline is this book: *Everyday Quantum Cookery*, by Delia Berry. She is the guru of all quantum cooks. She is able to conduct an investigation into the amazing world of elementary particles while at the same time whipping up a quick cheese omelette. Less skilful practitioners would get the two processes muddled and end up with a quick cheese particle and an elementary omelette, which would satisfy nobody. Moreover, Delia has made an amazing discovery in her kitchen laboratory: we already know that if you take two elementary particles and smash them together, you get released an amazing amount of energy – whereas, as Delia has demonstrated, if you take two cheese omelettes and smash *them* together, you get released an amazing amount of washing-up.

Another phenomenon that Delia has elucidated is gravity. How gravity works. Forget Newton. Forget Einstein. Delia's fundamental insight into the nature of gravity is how amazingly simple it is to create. As she explains, to make gravity all you need to do is take two spoonfuls of instant gravity granules, pour on boiling water, mix in some gluon stock – making sure it has the correct spin – and lo and behold, gravity springs miraculously into existence, manifesting itself at the bottom of the saucepan as a brown sludge. Amazing! Moreover, something that neither Newton nor Einstein grasped but Delia has discerned is the existence of different *varieties* of gravity. She has identified, among others, beef gravity, chicken gravity, and even gravity suitable for vegans. Vegan gravity. So if you are a vegan, concerned by the olfactory attraction of roast beef and pork sausages, you can now switch to the gravity of lentils, couscous and root vegetables – a much weaker attractive force, as all meat eaters will agree.

But – and this is important – all of us do need to ensure that we are partaking of the form of gravity appropriate to our lifestyle – and if you ever find yourself mysteriously floating away from the surface of the Earth, it will be because you're using the wrong sort of gravity granules...or possibly ingesting the wrong sort of mushrooms. Naughty!

That's all for now. In the next programme we will be looking at yet another new and amazing discipline which combines cooking with the evolution of life itself. The title of that programme will be *How to Make Primordial Soup*. See you then! Amazing!

Apocalypse Then

(Enter a team leader.)

Okay, everyone, okay! I would like to call this meeting to order. Thank you. Good evening, everyone, and welcome. We are gathered here as the designated members of the Apocalypse Planning Executive, SpearHeading Implementation Taskforce, or APESHIT for short. I hope everyone is here whose presence has been foretold, but I do need to check.

Whore of Babylon – is the Whore of Babylon present? Ah, good – hello, Whore. Yes, yes, do carry on with whatever, or indeed whomever, it is that you are carrying on with. Don't let me…distract you…

The Ten-Headed Beast – has the Beast with Ten Heads manifested himself yet? Ah, there you are…pretty unmistakable…hello, Beast! Hello, Beast! Hello, hello, hello, hello, hello, hello, hello and…hello! Beast, you've not been to one of these meetings before, have you, so has anyone given you the, uh, heads-up? Excellent. And do you know everyone here? You're on nodding terms with them all – jolly good.

The Four Horsemen of the Apocalypse – that's Pestilence, Death, War and Famine… Hello, are you with us? Four Horsemen? No? Three Horsemen? Two? Any of you? How about Horse*women* of the Apocalypse? No? L? G? B? T? Q…I…of the Apocalypse? We're an equal opportunities outfit, you know. No? None of them present? No worries, it's not the end of the world…no, hang on, it *is* the end of the world – that's the whole point. So we do need the four Horsemen.

Has anyone seen Pestilence? He's usually all over the place…yes, you, do *you* know where Pestilence is? He's what? What with? A *headache?* He's got a *headache?* So basically you're telling me that Pestilence is pulling a sickie? How exactly do you know this? I mean, who are you? Uh-huh…. And since when have the Horsemen of the Apocalypse had deputies? Oh, very well, but if you're not Pestilence himself but his deputy, what exactly is your designation? I mean, when you mount your mighty steed and go riding off throughout the world, foreshadowing a thousand years of terror, what exactly will you be spreading, if not pestilence? … *Man flu?* So you're going to be sweeping across the world, are you, thundering from continent to continent, and wherever your horse's hooves touch down, there will be a mighty outbreak of…*man flu?* The entire male population will be whingeing about little sniffles and sneezes? Hmm. No change there, then.

What about Death? What's happened to Death? Death is meant to be ever-present! Yes, and who are you? *Death's* deputy? So where is Death? *What?* Why has he got a day off…and what, exactly, is a 'Working Time Directive of the European Union'? APESHIT is *not* a member of the European Union and never has been: we merely act in an advisory role… Anyway, as Death's deputy, what is your actual designation? *Hangover?* Oh, excuse me – *Well Bad Hangover?* Oh, that's all right, then! And as you go sweeping through the continents, leaving well bad hangovers in your wake, people are bound to mistake you for Death, aren't they? Apart from the giveaway fact that twenty-four hours later they discover that they haven't actually died.

I now ask, with a sense of foreboding, what has happened to War? Yes, you? No, no, don't tell me, War can't make it but you are his deputy? Yeah, yeah, I'm psychic… So why isn't War here? *What?* Since when has War needed to go on a course of anger management? Give me strength… The whole *point* of war is that anger *isn't* managed. We don't want it managed, do we? So what is your designation as Death's deputy? *Constructive Criticism?* You intend to inaugurate a thousand years of terror by unleashing the demonic forces of…satisfaction ratings and online customer feedback forms? Oh, on a scale of one to ten – how terribly threatening!

Right, now, the Fourth Horseman is allegedly Famine, but I'm not holding my breath… Yes? You are Famine's deputy? And what exactly is *your* designation? What will *you* be unleashing throughout the peoples of the world, causing them to cry out in horror and despair, gnash their teeth and long for the end of days? … What? Tofu? *Tofu!* You'll be spreading *tofu* throughout the world?

That's more like it! Humankind will truly go…apeshit!

Gentlemen – and Whore of Babylon – we're in business!

High Wycombe

(Two TV presenters standing side by side on a rostrum: one speaks the italicised words, the other speaks the rest.)

High, Wycombe! and a big *Harlow* to all you *Peebles* out there. Our names are *Sid Cup* and *Stan Sted*, and we're *Dorking* to you about a new *Anglesey* on how to keep fit and *Wells*. There's *Moretonhampstead* all this than you would *Crediton*. So *Liskeard* to what we *Telford*, and remember, always exercise *Caerphilly*, *Leicester* you strain a *Mousehole*.

Right. *Firth of Forth*, when you *Wakefield* in the *Morecambe*, and have used the *Bognor*, if you're feeling *Lustleigh* why not go for a *Bude* swim at the local *Poole*? But *Watchet*! Don't be a *Birkenhead*! You shouldn't *Dawlish Longdown* there, in case you get a *Paignton* in your *Porlock*.

Be on your *Fishguard* for that sort of *Tring*, because I know a man who *Hatherleigh* large *Totnes* on his *Winkleigh*, right in the *Middlesbrough*, and you'll *Mevagissey* what happened to him. All of a *Sutton*, it *Turnham Green* and started to *Witheridge*. It really needed *Lancing*, but the surgeon *Whipsnade* off and he *Lostwithiel*. He is now fitted with a *Bolt-on Tintagel*, amongst other *Devizes*, but he still walks with a *Lympstone*, and he can't even *Widecombe in the Moor*. Let alone *Bovver Tracey*.

Oh *Hull!* Is that the *Thames?* We must hurry a-*Weymouth* to help *Virginia Water Bury St Edmunds*. So be good, *Beaworthy*. And have a *Great Yarmouth!*

Chudleigh Knighton to the lot of you.

Evans

(Enter a football commentator.)

Good afternoon and welcome to *Match of the Day*, and tonight we feature the annual contest between the two Welsh villages of Merthyr Matics, famous for its mining, and Merthyr Lated, famous for its ghosts or...er... merthyrlated spirits...

This is always a hard-fought contest, and the match should be starting any moment now. And here comes the referee, Evans, accompanied by his two linesmen, Evans and Evans. They're followed onto the pitch by the Merthyr Lated team, led by their captain, Evans. Many of you may not be familiar with these players, so I'll identify some of them for you. Number 3, standing in the middle of the pitch, is Evans; number 6, doing stretching exercises on the touchline, is Evans; number 7 over there is the new signing, Evans; number 10, coming out of the tunnel, is Vladimir Kalshstock...no, sorry, I can't read my own writing – his name is, in fact, Evans.

They're followed out by the Merthyr Matics team, led by their captain, Evans. And with both teams now in position, they are ready to start. The whistle goes, and they're off! But the referee brings them back on to play the game... Evans kicks off, and the ball is well taken by Evans, who passes to Evans, who passes to Evans, but it's nicely intercepted by Evans, who tries to pass to Evans, but the ball goes into touch! Evans collects the ball and Evans throws to Evans, who passes to Evans, who crosses to Evans, who dribbles to Evans, who kicks to Evans, who heads to Evans, who shoots!

Oh, he missed! Evans gathers the ball and boots it upfield to Evans. And now Evans is on the move: he beats Evans, beats Evans, beats Evans, beats Evans, beats Vladimir Kalshtock, beats Evans, beats Evans, but here comes Evans! And Evans is tackling Evans, and Evans is on the ground! He's writhing on the ground!… And here comes the referee…he's taking someone's name… it's *Evans*! He's taking *Evans'* name! This is a disgrace! This lad Evans – always in trouble.

A penalty has been awarded which Evans is going to take – and the defensive wall gets into position with Evans, Evans, Evans, Evans, Vladimir Kalshtock and Evans! Evans steadies himself, runs up…and it's a goal! A beautiful goal! What a goal! It was an 'eaven-sent opportunity and he took it! And here comes the rest of the team, and they're hugging him…and kissing him…and squeezing him…and…yergh! Ugh! And here comes the ref with a bucket of cold water! That's more like it.

But I've just been informed that this sort of behaviour breaches broadcasting guidelines and is not suitable for a pre-watershed audience, so regrettably I must hand you back to the studio and Dai Evans. So it's goodbye from me and good Evans from them.

After All

After All

"After all," said the young man with unfashionably long hair and a close-fitting beard, "in the long run, there's absolutely no hope of saving the planet. Is there?" He leaned back in his chair, crossed his arms in a definitive manner and looked round the room. This was the first time he had spoken, while the others, for the past half an hour or more, had waxed indignant about climate change, environmental pollution, species loss, fossil fuels and carbon footprints.

An annoyed babble broke out.

"That's just defeatist talk," a woman with a colourful crocheted shawl round her shoulders said indignantly. "What are you doing here if that's what you think?"

"Oh, don't get me wrong," said the young man, uncrossing his arms and leaning forward again. "I'm all for saving the whale and the Amazon rainforest, and installing solar panels and recycling and everything like that. Of course I am. But in the long run, the very long run, the very *very* long run, it won't be enough to save the planet. The trouble is, *nothing* will be enough. Or rather" —he seemed to consider the ambiguity of the last statement— "there's nothing that can be done that *will* be enough. In the long run."

"Nonsense!" An elderly man gesticulated with his walking stick. "If we all pull together we *can* do it. *All* of us, all round the world. Relentless pressure on every government in every country, make them see we mean business. Make them see it's in everyone's best interests, including theirs, to listen and *to act!*"

There were murmurs of agreement from everyone else – here, after all, was a veteran campaigner in all manner of causes over the decades. An inspiration to them all. Ban the Bomb. Anti-Apartheid. Section 28. Poll tax. The miners' strike. The Jarrow March, even – though, presumably, in a pram.

The young man shook his head. "Believe me," he said. "Even the most powerful government imaginable, one with total world control, would not, in the long run, be able to succeed."

"You're forgetting, young man," the veteran campaigner said in a finger-wagging tone, "that governments are susceptible to pressure, to persuasion and to protest. And to the fear of being overthrown! They have to listen! We shall overcome!"

A cheer went up. A little middle-aged man in a white linen suit and a panama hat started singing the protest song in a quavering voice, and then stopped.

"In the long run?" the young man said in response to the veteran campaigner.

"Precisely!" said the other.

"You keep using the expression 'in the long run'," a bespectacled woman remarked as she breastfed her baby. "What do you mean? How long is this 'long run'?"

"It's difficult to be precise," said the young man, leaning back again. "But probably something between three and a half billion years and five billion years. Give or take."

The veteran campaigner banged his walking stick on the floor. "Five years? What nonsense!"

"*Billion* years," the young man corrected him. "Around three and a half to five *billion* years."

"What are you talking about?" shawl woman demanded.

"The laws of nature," said the young man. "If I may explain?" He held up a hand, and such was his air of authority that the renewed babble died away. "Think about the Sun," he continued. "All the energy we use on Earth ultimately derives from it – apart from a spot of natural radioactivity. All life is dependent on absorbing and using the Sun's energy either directly or indirectly. When we burn coal or oil or gas for heating and lighting and making electricity, or use petrol and diesel in cars and so forth, we're using energy that was radiated by the Sun way back in time and was trapped in the formation of chemical bonds by trees and plants. But – and this is the point – the Sun is running down."

"Nonsense!" the veteran campaigner objected.

"I'm afraid it isn't. Don't be fooled into thinking that wind energy and solar energy and wave energy are *literally* renewable resources. They merely *seem* to be renewable because the Sun continues to pump out heat and light day after day as it has been doing for a good few billion years. But that doesn't mean its energy is inexhaustible. After all, the Sun is basically one vast nuclear reactor in which hydrogen atoms fuse together to make helium, releasing energy as they do so, and once a couple of hydrogen atoms have combined, that's it. It's an irreversible reaction. Which means that every day more of the Sun's fuel is used up. Its energy is slowly running out."

The young man paused for a drink of water, but nobody spoke – not even the veteran campaigner. The baby at the breast appeared to be listening intently. An earnest-looking schoolgirl of fourteen or fifteen cautiously opened her bag, took out a book and started thumbing through the pages near the end. It was a Bible.

The young man continued. "No matter how often we recycle our paper, switch off our energy-efficient light bulbs, eat organic carrots and jog to work instead of driving – no matter how much we do all these things, it doesn't make a jot of difference to the rate at which the Sun burns its fuel. And the day will come when it will have used up all its fuel. But, long before that happens, it will have entered another phase of its life cycle. In about three and a half billion years' time it will have become much hotter, rendering the Earth completely uninhabitable. It won't be only the tropical rainforests that will vanish, but all oceans, deserts, plains, peatbogs, mountains, valleys, ice caps, along with all the creatures that live therein, thereon and thereunder! The whole lot. That'll be nothing to do with pollution, holes in the ozone layer, greenhouse gases, farting cows, or the failure of governments to invest in bottle banks. It'll be because of the inexorable laws of nature. Physics. And in the next phase of the Sun's journey to ultimate extinction it will become a 'red giant', expanding and engulfing the inner planets, including the Earth in all likelihood. But the Earth will be dead long before that happens. Reduced to a mere cinder."

The silence in the room continued. Two or three present were scribbling notes, the others were staring morosely at the young man – all except for the veteran campaigner who stared angrily at the floor, the shawl woman who had covered her face with her crochet work, and breastfeeding woman, whose cheek was pressed against her baby's head.

Then the man in a white linen suit spoke. "But you're forgetting the ingenuity of mankind—"

"*Hu*mankind," breastfeeding woman interrupted.

"My apologies," he quavered. "The ingenuity of humankind. Long before all that happens, surely we will have colonised the galaxy – astronomers are discovering more and more planets which have conditions suitable for us to survive and, indeed, flourish on."

"Possibly," the young man conceded. "But supposing humankind does devise ways to travel to far distant parts of the galaxy, or even to other galaxies? Suppose that by the time our sun goes critical, *Homo sapiens*, with or without all the other species we're desperate to save, has colonised some other planet orbiting some other star? Another sun. So what? That star also has a limited lifespan, as have all the stars, and they're going to wink out, one by one, until there's not a single star left shining anywhere. The universe will have died. It'll have become simply a dead, sterile, infinite expanse of nothingness, void of life."

"Bloody hell, you're a cheerful Charlie," someone muttered when it was evident the young man had finished speaking.

"Excuse me," the schoolgirl said diffidently, "but aren't you forgetting God?"

"I don't think so," said the young man in kindly fashion. "But would you like to explain a little more?"

"It says in the Bible, in the Book of Revelation..." And she read out, blushing furiously, as one who hates speaking out in a group but feels compelled to do so, "'I saw a new heaven and a new earth; for the first heaven and the first earth had passed away.' Couldn't that mean that – well, when this one comes to an end, God will create a new universe?"

"I'm afraid," the young man said, still speaking kindly, "I'm not able to comment with any authority on religious or metaphysical matters – although it does seem to me that if God is going to sort it all out in the end like that, then human endeavour to change things now is superfluous."

"I hadn't thought of that," the schoolgirl admitted. She looked downcast.

"It's an interesting point, though," the young man said encouragingly. "Thank you for mentioning it."

The schoolgirl blushed some more, but said nothing further.

"So are you saying that we should do nothing," white linen man asked, "either because one day billions of years into the future the Earth won't exist, and the universe will become what you said it would, or because God will sort it all out, as our young friend suggests?"

"No!" The young man spoke decisively. "Of course not. After all" —he gestured towards the baby who, well fed, was now oblivious to her eventual fate— "we don't see that baby and say, 'well, everyone dies one day, so there's no point in caring for her now', do we? Or 'let's leave it to God to care for her'. No, we don't. We say we should do what we can to make sure she and everyone else lives as good and happy a life as is possible, however long or short that life may turn out to be. And we do that by caring for each other as much as we can. The Earth is like that baby. But however much we do care, we can't get away from the fact that each and every one of us, from babes in arms to senior citizens, ultimately has an appointment with death, and so does the Earth itself. And so does this universe, whatever God might or might not choose to do subsequently."

"I suppose, then," the veteran campaigner broke in sarcastically, "we shouldn't be petitioning governments to do things differently, we should be petitioning God?"

"It's an idea!" the young man smiled. "But I doubt it would get us very far. No, it's up to us to do what we can, but also to be prepared to accept the inevitable. Anyway" —he stood up— "I'm afraid I need to go now. *Tempus fugit.* Many thanks for your time and attention. Good evening."

The babble resumed as the young man left the room.

They broke for coffee, and when they reconvened they returned to the main business of the meeting. Though generally agreed that the young man's speech had been interesting and thought-provoking, it mustn't, as the veteran campaigner insisted, deflect them from the serious task of tackling the current menace of single-use plastic. For even if the young man were right that the day would dawn when the entire Earth would be roasted by the Sun, followed a few billion years later by the universe itself ending up inert and void of all life, so (to use his dismissive expression) what?

There was not much they could do about *that*, after all…

Also by R. N. F. Skinner

Still Crazy...

A dinner party. A cabaret. The unforgotten past bursts into the present, ripping open the future.

When Phil, an undergraduate at Cambridge University, performs in cabaret at a party, he meets and falls in love with Melanie. As she in turn appears to have fallen in love with him, he cannot understand why she then plays hard to get, even after he learns of the traumatic events that shaped her teenage years. But the influence of former boyfriend Simon is still strong, and she and Phil part. Twenty-five years later, both now married, they meet again by chance and resume their relationship. Soon each faces a tough choice: will Melanie decide on love or loyalty? Will Phil commit to his estranged wife or return to his first love?

Spanning forty-two years, and interweaving three time strands set in Cambridge, Devon and London, the story of Phil and Melanie also tracks the highs and lows of performing comedy in cabaret; the compatibility of science and religion in bed; moments of transcendence; the precariousness of mental health; ambiguous adjectives; climbing Skiddaw; and transgressive ducks.

"This is a wonderful novel, beautifully written, that threads its way through the lives and loves of its characters who step vividly out of the pages. A delight to read." *The Rt Hon Lord Smith of Finsbury, Master of Pembroke College, Cambridge*

Still Crazy... (SilverWood 2020) can be ordered from bookshops, or online.
Kindle/e-book version also available.

ISBN 978-1-78132-991-7   RRP £11.99

www.ingramcontent.com/pod-product-compliance
Lightning Source LLC
Chambersburg PA
CBHW031233260626
47169CB00007B/2276